PRINCE DUSTIN
AND
CLARA

SECRETS OF THE BLACK FOREST
BOOK TWO

PRINCE DUSTIN
AND
CLARA

SECRETS OF THE BLACK FOREST
BOOK TWO

by

DANIEL LEE NICHOLSON

Fossil Mountain Publishing, LLC

FOSSIL
MOUNTAIN PUBLISHING

ACKNOWLEDGMENTS

Fossil Mountain Publishing would like to thank the dance, performing and fine arts communities for their commitment to providing excellence in instruction and their devotion to inspiring our youth.

There is no limit to what a person can do that has been inspired by *The Arts*!

Printed in the United States of America

First Edition / Hardcover

Library of Congress Control Number: 2019932439

ISBN-13: 978-0-9986191-4-9 (Hardcover)
ISBN-13: 978-0-9986191-3-2 (Paperback)

Fossil Mountain Publishing
PO BOX 48092
Watauga, TX 76148

www.FossilMountainPublishing.com

for John and Nathan

McKenzie

TABLE OF CONTENTS

SECRETS OF THE BLACK FOREST
BOOK TWO

Prologue

-PROLOGUE-

The Wizard

On a splendid spring day many, many years ago, the remaining snow on the mountaintops finally melted. The last of the rock-hard icicles surrendered. They were no match against the warm, gentle breeze in the air. Gushing water rushed down the side of the mountain. The water landed in every crease and crevice, as if trying to hold on, trying to escape crashing below.

For centuries people assumed the Black Forest got its name from the perpetual darkness created by the canopy of evergreen trees that block the sunlight. However, the inhabitants that live *deeper* in the Black Forest know otherwise. There is a reason why the land is called the Black Forest, *and those that venture deeper into its woods, seldom return to tell their tales.*

❖ ❖ ❖

A mysterious old man lives in an even older mill deep in the Black Forest – *the old mill has many secrets.* The old man is known by all as Herr Drosselmeyer. Wearing black from head to toe, Drosselmeyer is an ominous sight to see. It is assumed he doesn't have a change of clothes because he is always seen wearing a swinging black cape, rumpled top hat, and a black patch that covers his left eye.

Legend has it that Drosselmeyer lost his eye while engaged in battle, fighting a giant mouse of human proportions. The eye not covered by the black patch is pale blue, almost white–ghastly white.

Other than being, *the best toymaker in all the Black Forest*, the cottage people know little about Herr Drosselmeyer. His age is also a mystery. For generations, elders of the land would tell tales of Herr Drosselmeyer and Helmut, the dog that was always by his side. The dog doesn't appear to age either.

Whatever the cottage people thought of Herr Drosselmeyer, *it was far from the truth.*

❖ ❖ ❖

On this splendid day, Drosselmeyer was deep in thought. He glared out of the parlor window of the old mill at the glimmering lake. His long slender nose and gaunt cheeks reflected off the window. His gray hair almost reached his shoulders.

A small blue bird with large white wings appeared and rapped at the window.

Tap-Tap   *Tap-Tap*   *Tap-Tap*

"Hello Herr Drosselmeyer!" the little bird said, flapping its wings for attention. Drosselmeyer smiled and waved at the little blue bird.

The little blue bird's eyes sparkled. "I learned some new dance steps, wanna see?" Without waiting for a reply, the little blue bird started spinning around and flapping its wings. Drosselmeyer clapped.

The little blue bird then fluttered backward. It looked like it was flying in the wrong direction. *"Wheee!"* the little blue bird exclaimed. Herr Drosselmeyer nodded approvingly with a smile.

The little blue bird then shook its wings and tapped its feet. "I can dance, just like *them*!" Herr Drosselmeyer clapped with a nod, as if saying, bravo.

"I've gotta go now," the little blue bird said. It then disappeared–the bird vanished.

POOF! The little blue bird was gone.

Moments later, Drosselmeyer was again deep in thought. He recounted back to last Christmas Eve. *I wish things had gone differently*, he thought. Drosselmeyer hung his head. Helmut barked softly, as though he could understand Drosselmeyer's thoughts. Drosselmeyer turned and smiled at the dog.

Last Christmas Eve, Dr. Stahlbaum and his wife, Katharina, hosted their annual holiday party. The Stahlbaums lived in a town just outside the Black Forest. Every year Herr Drosselmeyer would make toys at his old mill for the Stahlbaum's children, twelve-year-old Clara, and seven-year-old Fritz. The toys would do amazing things, entertaining all the guests. However, last year was different—*very different.*

Drosselmeyer gave Clara a very *special toy*. It wasn't really a toy, at all. Clara would later discover the secret of her gift.

As Drosselmeyer looked out the window of the old mill, all the cuckoo birds in the cuckoo clocks that lined the walls of his parlor, hundreds upon hundreds of clocks, spun out of their doors. With a high-pitched cackle, the birds cuckooed. It sounded like they were singing off-key.

CUCKOO   CUCKOO   CUCKOO

The sound bounced off the walls of the parlor. Although Helmut covered his ears with his front paws, Drosselmeyer seemed unnerved. Herr Drosselmeyer simply glanced at the clocks and then stared back out the window at the lake.

Drosselmeyer leaned against the windowsill, again deep in thought. Last Christmas Eve, Queen Nordika had captured Egon, King of the Mice, and locked Egon away in her dungeon at the Ice Palace.

Queen Nordika, the Snow Queen, had a massive and fierce army. Only the army of Konfetenburg was larger. Drosselmeyer considered, *When Prince Dustin is crowned King of Konfetenburg, he will have a strong influence over the other kingdoms in the Black Forest.*

Suddenly, Drosselmeyer stiffened. Helmut must have sensed something too because the dog started barking and gritting its teeth. Drosselmeyer had a vision. He shuddered.

The vision took Drosselmeyer inside a castle, *deeper in the Black Forest.* Drosselmeyer stepped back sharply. His face shone with worry. Beads of sweat trickled from his brow. Helmut barked louder and *LOUDER.* Herr Drosselmeyer shook his head. He tried to look at the face of the man in his vision, but the man's face was hidden from his view.

"Clara!" Drosselmeyer exclaimed in a deep voice. Helmut howled and jumped around in circles like a spinning top.

Drosselmeyer then ran out of the parlor. Helmut charged behind him.

A sense of doom filled the air. The doors of the cuckoo clocks flung open. This time, the cuckoo birds did not spin out. They remained in the safety of their chambers.

End of Prologue

Queen Nordika, the Snow Queen, felt danger in the air!

ACT 1

-1-

Fritz

Fritz whispered, "If we tip-toe, Clara won't hear us." Peering through tousled hair from an overdue haircut, Fritz looked back at his friend Bruno. The boys slowly crept out of Fritz's bedroom.

Bruno nodded. He seemed just as eager as Fritz. Without turning around, Fritz pulled a toy soldier out of his pants pocket and flung it. With a soft plop, it landed on his bed. The little white mouse Fritz kept in a cage by his bed squealed and jumped.

SQUEAK   *SQUEAK*   *SQUEAK*

"She always tells my Mom. She thinks I might get hurt or something," Fritz said, waving his hand dismissively.

"I'm glad I don't have a big sister," Bruno said, shaking his head.

"Ahh, she's all right, just a scaredy cat." Fritz and Bruno peeped down the hall. "I heard her go in her room earlier," Fritz said softly, nodding in the direction of Clara's bedroom. The boys stood still and cocked their heads. Their eyes sparkled with excitement. Fritz signaled Bruno forward. A quiet shushing sound could be heard as the boys made their way down the hall toward the grand staircase.

❖ ❖ ❖

It was the middle of May and school was out of session. With Fritz's friend Bruno staying over, Clara decided to spend the remainder of the week over her best friend's house. *Fritz and Bruno won't be able to annoy me while I'm at Marie's*, Clara reasoned.

The sun glowed in soft shades of amber. Clara was making her bed and fluffing the over-stuffed pillows. Her bedroom was decorated in ballet pink with white lace accents on the bed skirt and curtains. A warm breeze from the open window gently blew the curtains in rhythm. The smell of primroses scented the air. Clara's chestnut-colored hair bounced as she tugged at her bed linen. She smiled as she gently positioned the toe shoes that were hanging on her bedpost. Clara scanned the room. *It's clean*, she said under her breath.

Clara walked over to her rocking chair. She smiled and lifted a doll that was sitting on the chair. The boy doll was dressed in a blue and red soldier's uniform. Clara held the doll like it was a real person. She then gently placed the doll on one of the fluffy pillows on her bed. She stared at the doll as if she expected the doll to speak.

All of a sudden, Clara jerked her head. She thought she heard something coming from down the hall. After a few moments, not hearing anything further, she turned back and sat down on her bed. The bed creaked from her weight. *I'll be glad when mother and father return*, Clara thought.

Clara's father and mother, Dr. and Mrs. Stahlbaum, had been away for two weeks, providing medical treatment to people that lived in a small village, far away from Clara's hometown. Although Clara's mother had no medical training, Katharina had a very soothing nature, so she joined Dr. Stahlbaum.

Clara lifted the soldier doll and looked into its eyes. "Prince Dustin, would you like to go with me to Marie's house?" Of course, there was no response. It remained as stiff as a board, *or doll.*

❖ ❖ ❖

Mrs. Koch, the head cook and housekeeper, and Mr. Godfrey, the Stahlbaum's butler and head of house staff were in charge of the household while Dr. and Mrs. Stahlbaum were away.

"I haven't seen the boys since breakfast," Mrs. Koch said in a flat tone. Mr. Godfrey shrugged his shoulders.

Standing with her fists balled on her hips, Mrs. Koch continued, "Never have I seen two boys eat that much food."

Mr. Godfrey gulped and avoided eye contact with Mrs. Koch.

"I expected to have some of the sausage as leftovers for lunch ... and Clara didn't get any cinnamon rolls," Mrs. Koch said. "I went upstairs to tell Clara breakfast was ready, and by the time I came back down, all the food was gone." Mrs. Koch continued in a disgusted tone, "Those boys reeked of cinnamon."

Mr. Godfrey swallowed as he reached for a large bowl on the top shelf in the cupboard. He quickly handed it to Mrs. Koch. Mrs. Koch snatched the bowl from Mr. Godfrey. "If those boys eat like this the rest of the week, I'm gonna have to send Amalie back to the market."

Mr. Godfrey changed subjects. In his deep voice, Mr. Godfrey said, "What time is

Marie and her mother picking Clara up this evening?"

"At seven," Mrs. Koch replied. Her voice had returned to normal. "Let me go check on Clara. I need to make sure she packs her warm sweater. It still gets cold in the evenings you know." Mrs. Koch rushed out of the kitchen and waddled up the back staircase.

Mr. Godfrey rubbed his nose. Cinnamon could be smelled on his fingertips. He quickly stepped over to the sink and washed his hands.

❖ ❖ ❖

Fritz and Bruno stopped at the top of the grand staircase. The staircase was the centerpiece of the Stahlbaum's foyer. It was slightly curved with a smooth handrail that curled under at the end. Every day, the house staff polished the handrail until it was shiny and slick.

"I bet I beat ya!" Fritz looked down the staircase with eager eyes.

"I bet not," Bruno replied.

"I bet I beat ya, *face-first*!" Fritz mounted the left banister, face-first, gripping the handrail.

Bruno gulped. Anxiety could be seen in his eyes. He straddled the top of the right banister, face-first.

"On the count of three," Fritz said. He quickly glanced over at Bruno. Bruno glanced back at Fritz. Bruno nodded with excitement, no longer looking frightened.

"One," Fritz said, gripping the handrail with his knees. His eyes glistened with excitement as he stared at the bottom of the banister.

"T-w-o," Fritz said slowly. Bruno shot Fritz a glance then gripped the banister with his knees. Both boys looked animated, with wide eyes and flashy grins that showed all their teeth.

"...and three!" Fritz screamed. He immediately loosened his knees and slid down the banister.

WHOOSH

Bruno shouted, "Whoa!" as he let loose his grip, and slid down the other banister.

WHOOSH

It was quick. Fritz's heart pounded in his chest. He held his head low and made sure his knees did not touch the railing, so he could glide faster. Faster and faster Fritz slid.

Fritz was now at the curve in the staircase. He almost slid off. WHOOSH! Fritz skimmed the curve of the banister. Fritz sailed down even faster. Faster and faster he slid.

Then just as quickly, it was over.

THUMP

Fritz landed with a thump on top of a soft rug at the bottom of the staircase. Seconds later, he heard Bruno fall right next to him.

Fritz clenched both his hands and thrust them in the air, relishing the victory. "Yes!" Fritz yelled.

Fritz's face gleamed as he looked over at Bruno. Fritz noticed that Bruno was not smiling. Bruno was staring with a stone face at something behind Fritz.

Fritz swallowed and turned his head slowly, hesitating. He looked in the direction that Bruno was staring.

Mr. Godfrey shook his head as he glared at Fritz. Fritz looked up at Mr. Godfrey with *that innocent look* that he had every time he got into trouble. It worked most times.

Mr. Godfrey looked the boys over. They were in one piece, no broken parts.

After seeing that the boys were not hurt, Mr. Godfrey scolded them for sliding down the banisters. He reminded them of how dangerous it could be. The boys promised not to do it again.

Mr. Godfrey then whisked the boys out the foyer. "Hurry, she's coming," Mr. Godfrey said, rather frantically. He rushed the boys into the parlor. Fritz and Bruno's eyes went wide. "If Mrs. Koch finds out you slid down the banisters, I won't hear the end of it. Now go," Mr. Godfrey said. Fritz and Bruno bolted out of sight. They sounded like horses across the hardwood floors.

Mr. Godfrey shook his head.

❖ ❖ ❖

"I could take this sweater. Mother bought it for me last year. It still fits," Clara said, holding up a blue sweater. Before Mrs. Koch could respond, a commotion could be heard coming from downstairs.

Mrs. Koch raised her shoulders and turned her head toward Clara's bedroom door. "What are those boys up to now?" Mrs. Koch said. Not waiting for an answer, she hurried out of Clara's bedroom. Clara lagged behind with a curious look. *What is Fritz up to?*

Mrs. Koch walked past Fritz's bedroom. Without looking inside, she rushed down the hall toward the staircase.

Clara stopped in front of Fritz's bedroom. She saw the toy sword that her Uncle Drosselmeyer had given Fritz for Christmas. It was on the floor, along with most of Fritz's other toys. Clara stepped over the threshold into the bedroom, being careful not to trip over the toys. Just then, Fritz and Bruno darted into the bedroom, out of breath.

Fritz collided with Clara almost knocking her down.

"Sorry, Clara," Fritz said, panting.

"What did you do?" Clara said, raising her voice. "What was all that noise?"

Fritz looked at Bruno. Bruno hung his head low.

"Uh, we were just having fun," Fritz said. Clara stared at Fritz, tapping her foot, with her hand on her hip. "We, uhm–" Fritz paused. Clara narrowed her eyes, as if telling Fritz to continue. "We slid down the banisters," Fritz said, as he avoided looking at Clara.

Clara's eyes widened. "You know mother doesn't want you sliding down the banisters." Clara looked Fritz and Bruno over before continuing. In a concerned tone, Clara said, "You could get hurt."

"We're fine," Fritz said, looking at Bruno. Bruno nodded in agreement.

Clara looked at both of the boys with her left brow raised. "Mrs. Koch is looking for Mr. Godfrey to find out what you did."

Fritz swallowed, and Bruno's eyes bulged.

"She's going to blame Mr. Godfrey when she finds out. She'll probably fuss at him all night."

Fritz lowered his eyes.

"I have to finish packing," Clara said. "Please stay out of trouble." Clara stared at each of them, waiting for a response.

"We will," Fritz finally said.   Clara turned and left.

As Fritz closed his bedroom door behind Clara, his face lit up. He rubbed his chin, raised his left brow and nodded his head at Bruno.

With a sneaky grin, Fritz said, *"I know what we can do!"*

-2-

Queen Nordika

Queen Nordika, the Snow Queen, felt danger in the air! She usually enjoyed rides through the forest on her sleigh. In the springtime, wheels that swivel were added to her carriage, enabling it to whip through the grassy terrain at high speed.

Queen Nordika looked up. The smoke-gray sky looked as though it were holding tears of rain. "General, we must travel quickly," she said. The General was the leader of Queen Nordika's army of large white shepherd canines. The General was the largest and fiercest of them all.

"Yes, Your Highness." The General said and then crashed through the woods like lightning. The team of shepherds moved so swiftly the flowers became a blur. Queen Nordika was only able to smell their soft floral fragrance as they scented the air.

❖ ❖ ❖

Springtime is an enchanting time of year deep in the Black Forest. A carpet of bluebell flowers casts a purple glow across the meadows, while daffodils explode with bursts of sunshine. Brilliant scarlet-colored flowers that look like poppies intoxicate all that wander a little too close, *but by then it is often too late.*

In the Black Forest, everyone calls Queen Nordika, the Snow Queen. She lives in a palace that is shrouded in ice crystals that sparkles with prisms of color in the winter. She is always dressed in white flowing silk that blends in with her skin tone and hair. In soft all-white attire, Queen Nordika could look like a ghost, from a far distance.

Although elegant and graceful, Queen Nordika is a fierce protector of the animals and creatures that inhabit the Black Forest. Few have ever challenged her, and those that have quickly regretted their actions.

❖ ❖ ❖

As Queen Nordika, the General, and the team of shepherd lieutenants in her army, traveled through the forest, Evergreens rustled, and their pine needles bristled. Pine cones fell to the ground like confetti. However, no animals were seen, not even heard. Birds were not singing, owls were not hooting, and bobcats were not crying. The forest was *dead* silent.

As they passed a winding river, its current became violent, as if it wanted to get Queen Nordika's attention, as if it wanted to warn her. *Something is not right*, Queen Nordika sensed.

The General moved his head sharply from left to right. He has been in many battles, losing none. His senses were especially keen. He could sniff danger from creatures and animals above and below ground.

The General and his lieutenants weaved between the trees at a speed that typically they could only reach on fresh snow. The canines, all but the General, tossed and turned their torsos erratically.

I must get to Prince Dustin and Princess Leyna before it's too late. Queen Nordika grimaced. Ever since their parents, King Marc and Queen Arabelle, went missing, Queen Nordika kept a protective eye over Prince Dustin and Princess Leyna.

Queen Nordika could now see the gates of the Kingdom of Konfetenburg in the distance. Everyone called the Kingdom of Konfetenburg, the Land of Sweets. Fir and Spruce evergreen trees surrounded its perimeter.

A massive castle, built of logs, was the centerpiece of the kingdom. It was humbly called the Log Cabin Castle of Konfetenburg. The castle's stained-glass windows shimmered like candy wrappers. Smaller log cabin structures dotted the land behind the castle. Water flowed freely underneath wooden bridges connecting the structures, like an endless path.

Mountains draped the land in the distance, like a fortress, as though they were watching over Konfetenburg, protecting it. Once inside the gates, a blanket of tranquility was immediately felt by all.

There was a flurry of activity when Queen Nordika arrived at the Land of Sweets. Today, Prince Dustin would be crowned King of Konfetenburg. All the dignitaries of nearby kingdoms would attend the festive affair. Queen Nordika quickly surveyed the area. "Nothing appears strange," she said softly to the General.

Queen Nordika was held in the highest esteem. Everyone moved aside, making space for her carriage. And of course, as Queen Nordika and the General stepped toward the Log Cabin Castle, there was the usual small talk that one would expect at such affairs:

"Good day, Queen Nordika, you are looking ever so lovely."

"Beautiful day for a coronation, do you not agree, Queen Nordika?"

"I believe Prince Dustin will be the youngest King in all of the Black Forest. He turned fifteen today, you know."

"King Marc and Queen Arabelle would have been so proud of Prince Dustin. I mean, well, the King and Queen could return ...."

"And I must say that it was quite benevolent of them to adopt Princess Sugar Plum into their family. She's just a couple of years younger than Prince Dustin."

"I heard that Prince Dustin and Princess Sugar Plum searched the entire forest for King Marc and Queen Arabelle."

"Except, deeper in the Black Forest."

"Oh, no! Hopefully, the King and Queen did not go there."

"That would explain why they never returned."

"Princess Nixie, we may want to avoid mentioning the King and Queen's disappearance tonight in front of Prince Dustin and Princess Sugar Plum."

"I heard that Princess Sugar Plum planned everything down to the smallest detail for the coronation."

"They say Princess Sugar Plum's dress was made from the finest spun silk of caterpillars."

"I can't wait to see it!"

Queen Nordika nodded at everyone as she and the General rushed inside the castle. Her silk scarf fell gently down to her shoulders and floated behind as she walked. Although she walked with haste, not a strand of her hair moved. Everybody bowed or curtsied seeing Queen Nordika. She smiled genuinely at everyone.

The aroma of sweet fresh-baked bread blended with the smell of creamy dark chocolate. Every surface held platters of scrumptious sweets of all kind. The Kingdom of Konfetenburg had the best bakers in all of the Black Forest, which is how it got its nickname, the *Land of Sweets*.

Biscuits for invited animals and creatures were overflowing in baskets on floors next to the tables. The General passed by the baskets without even a glance.

"Look for Prince Dustin," Queen Nordika said to the General. "We must alert him."

The General's pointed ears stood erect, and his saber-shaped tail stiffened. His penetrating eyes focused as he looked around the castle.

❖ ❖ ❖

Creeping inside the Log Cabin Castle, an old man dressed in all black almost looked like a shadow amongst the servants and guests. He shot a quick menacing glance at Queen Nordika and the General. They were walking toward the Grand Hall. It didn't appear that they noticed the man dressed in all black.

"It's her," the man cursed under his breath. Pulling at his swinging black cape, he ducked out of sight, covering his face with his rumpled top hat. The black patch covering his left eye could barely be seen.

I must stay clear of Nordika and that dog, the man thought. His stooped shoulders made his black cape seem even longer as he snuck around the corners of the Log Cabin Castle. Nobody seemed put off by the man dressed in all black. Everyone nodded at him as they passed.

The man reached the steps going down to the cellar. The light was dim as he stepped lower into the darkness, down the staircase. At the bottom of the staircase, he arrived at a long corridor. The old man then patted for something underneath his cape. The impression of a skeleton key took shape in the fabric. The man muttered with a scowl, "He better be there."

The creepy-looking old man continued down the corridor. "They won't know what's coming for them, after all I've been through— it is all his fault," the old man uttered.

The man noticed several doors along the walls of the corridor. He continued down the hall to the very last one. A table with a silver pitcher sat opposite the door. A lighted sconce glowed on the wall next to the table.

The old man wiped dust off the silver pitcher and looked at his reflection. He adjusted his rumpled top hat and then walked to the door. It had a brass lever and metal brackets.

❖ ❖ ❖

Upstairs in her chamber, Princess Leyna was preparing for the coronation. Everyone called Princess Leyna by her nickname, Princess Sugar Plum, or simply, Sugar Plum.

King Marc and Queen Arabelle, Prince Dustin's parents, adopted Sugar Plum when she was a baby. The Kingdom of Bosartig, the Land of Mice, ravaged the Kingdom of Fliegen, Princess Sugar Plum's homeland.

When King Marc's army arrived to thwart off the attack by the Mice, it was too late. He only found a small baby crying in a bassinet, hidden under a bush. Princess Sugar Plum was immediately adopted by King Marc and Queen Arabelle, becoming Prince Dustin's only sibling.

Prince Dustin, two years older than Princess Sugar Plum, was quite protective of his little sister. Even though Princess Sugar Plum was a *Tree Fairy*, and could fly from harm if she had enough notice, Prince Dustin still watched over her.

When Prince Dustin's parents vanished, Princess Sugar Plum asked the magical Great Tree in the Land of Fliegen to grant Prince Dustin the ability to fly, so that they could more easily search for their parents, King Marc and Queen Arabelle. Prince Dustin was then able to fly like Sugar Plum. However, their parents were never found.

❖ ❖ ❖

"Gertrude, is everything in place?" Princess Sugar Plum asked. "I want the orchestra to play the *March of Konfetenburg* as soon as Prince Dustin enters the Grand Hall."

"Yes, Princess Sugar Plum." Gertrude held tight to the vase of flowers in her arms. Gertrude was Princess Sugar Plum's assistant for the coronation ceremony. She helped Sugar Plum organize the day's activities. Princess Sugar Plum considered Gertrude, a friend.

"Do you think we have enough flowers in the Grand Hall? I want it to look beautiful," Princess Sugar Plum said while gently breathing the floral scent in the air. She smiled before hearing Gertrude's response.

"Yes, the Grand Hall looks quite beautiful and the flowers can be smelled throughout the castle. They smell almost as good as the Baumkuchen cake, but not quite." Both Gertrude and Princess Sugar Plum chuckled.

"I have a special dance that I plan to perform for the coronation," Princess Sugar Plum said. "I have been practicing all week."

"You dance so lovely, Princess Sugar Plum. Everyone will be delighted."

Princess Sugar Plum blushed. "Thank you, Gertrude." Tree fairies were known for their dancing abilities, and there was not a better dancer in all the Black Forest than Princess Sugar Plum. When she danced, magic seemed to happen. It was unexplainable.

"I want everything to be perfect for Prince Dustin. After he enters and takes his place on the stage, I will enter the hall to begin the festivities," Princess Sugar Plum said while twirling around the room, practicing her dance.

Gertrude smiled. "Everything should go smoothly."

"Can you let me know when Queen Nordika arrives? I am looking forward to seeing her," Princess Sugar Plum said.

Gertrude checked the cuckoo clock on the wall. "I was told just a little bit ago, that Queen Nordika's sleigh was approaching. You have time, you know whenever she arrives, everybody crowds around her."

Princess Sugar Plum nodded, still dancing.

"I wish Herr Drosselmeyer could have come. He seemed quite anxious when he spoke to Prince Dustin. He said something about a matter he had to take care of," Princess Sugar Plum said. Disappointment could be heard in her voice.

"Herr Drosselmeyer? I saw him near the Grand Hall before I came upstairs," Gertrude responded.

Princess Sugar Plum stopped dancing and smiled at Gertrude, "Good. I can't wait to see him! He must have taken care of the matter. Prince Dustin will be so pleased."

"I better go check on things downstairs. Do you need anything before I go?" Gertrude asked.

"I-I'm fine," Princess Sugar Plum responded with a stutter. *I hope I'm not forgetting anything*, she thought.

Princess Sugar Plum then rushed into her dressing room to finish getting dressed. She added another pin to her hair as she passed a mirror. Her reddish-brown, curly hair was styled in a high bun. The red color of her hair was partly the reason why she got her nickname, Princess Sugar Plum. Only Queen Nordika called Sugar Plum by her given name, Princess Leyna.

Princess Sugar Plum stepped into her dressing room. A magnificent tiara with pink crystals and bright gemstones could be seen in a glass case set on top of a pillar. The crown glistened from the sun's rays beaming through the windows. A rainbow of color danced across the walls of the room.

❖ ❖ ❖

The creepy-looking old man dressed in all black looked down the long corridor before turning the lever on the door in the cellar. The door seemed heavy. The man used his shoulder to push the door open. The metal hinges of the door squeaked. Once it was cracked enough, the man slipped through.

A corner of the man's cape got caught in the door jamb. The man yanked at the bottom of his cape and pulled it free. Using his shoulder, the man in all black closed the door behind him. He peeked out, just before the door was entirely shut. Seeming satisfied, the man shut the door. The man dressed in all black was now out of sight.

An eerie silence seemed to choke the air in the corridor.

-3-

Egon Returns

Mrs. Koch stomped back into Clara's bedroom with a disgusted look on her face. "Have you seen Mr. Godfrey? I looked all over for him?" Before Clara could respond, Mrs. Koch continued, shaking her index finger, "I told him that he had to keep an eye on those boys."

Clara smiled politely. She thought it best not to mention that she saw Mr. Godfrey just a few minutes earlier from her bedroom window. Mr. Godfrey had been walking fast, looking over his shoulder.

"Hmmph!" Mrs. Koch sighed. "When I find that Mr. Godfrey, he won't hear the end of this." Mrs. Koch added in a curious tone, "Those boys seem mighty quiet now."

Clara avoided eye contact with Mrs. Koch. She twisted her lip and cocked her head. *What is Fritz up to?* she wondered.

Mrs. Koch noticed the folded clothes on Clara's bed. "Dear Clara, I almost forgot that you are spending the rest of the week over Marie's. I'll let you finish packing." Mrs. Koch hugged Clara. "I'll find that Mr. Godfrey, and those boys."

"Yes, Mrs. Koch." Clara looked down at the floor. She knew that the boys would not stay out of trouble.

The sun shone high in the sky. Its rays filtered through the bedroom curtains. Clara glanced out her window. It was noon. The sun illuminated her toe shoes hanging from the bedpost. *Marie and I can practice our dancing,* she thought. Clara gently removed her toe shoes from the post. She continued packing. Clara no longer thought about Fritz or Bruno.

❖ ❖ ❖

A short time later, Clara finished packing. *This can barely close.* Clara sighed, stuffing her clothes into the small wooden case. A light clinking sound could be heard as Clara closed the brass latch. *Finally.*

Clara's stomach growled. It was well past lunchtime. She wondered what Mrs. Koch had prepared for their meal. She looked down the hall. Fritz's bedroom door was still closed. Clara thought it odd that she could not hear any sounds coming from Fritz's room. On the way toward the back staircase, Clara smelled garlic and onions and smiled. *Pot roast.*

In the kitchen, Clara saw bread puffs with powdered sugar sprinkled on top. She grabbed one and pulled it apart. White pudding oozed out. Clara gobbled it quickly, wiping the powder from her lips with the back of her hand.

Clara grabbed another one. This time she sat down to eat it. She giggled thinking about Mr. Godfrey and Mrs. Koch. She knew that Mr. Godfrey was going to hear it from Mrs. Koch when he returned. Clara finished off the roll then took the stairs up to her room.

When Clara made it back to her bedroom, she noticed that the sky was now overcast. *I hope it doesn't rain.* Clara sat down on her bed. She still had several hours before Marie would arrive to pick her up. *What am I forgetting?* Clara looked around her room. She remembered that she still needed to pack her hairbrush and ribbons. She wondered if she could squeeze anything else into her luggage.

Clara walked over to her dresser bureau thinking about the fun that she was going to have over Marie's house. Suddenly, Clara flinched. She heard something. *Something was in her room.*

Clara trembled. Clara remembered hearing that sound before, last Christmas Eve, when she was attacked—by the Mouse King.

Clara looked at her bedroom window. She hadn't noticed when she returned to her room, but the window was now closed. She had left it open before she went downstairs. *Maybe Mrs. Koch closed the window,* Clara hoped.

Clara's face turned white. She glanced around the room. Things felt out of place. She opened the box where she kept her hairbrush and ribbons. They were not inside the box. They were missing. *They're gone.* Clara backed away from the bureau covering her mouth. *I know I left them there.*

Something caught Clara's attention on the floor on the other side of the bed. She walked closer for a better look. As she stepped slower and slower, Clara saw her hair ribbons, along with her hairbrush, scattered on the floor.

Clara shrieked, "Oh no!" Clara looked at the pillow on her bed. She then stood still, paralyzed.

"Not again," Clara gasped looking at her bed. Her Nutcracker Soldier doll that she calls, Prince Dustin, was no longer there. *He's gone!*

Clara jerked. She heard a screeching - scratching - skittering sound coming from her closet. Clara cupped her ears. She didn't want to hear it. She didn't want to believe it.

It's happening again!

❖ ❖ ❖

Mr. Godfrey looked to his left, then to his right as he approached the front door of the Stahlbaum's mansion. He had been gone for some time. He hoped that Mrs. Koch was busy and had forgotten about the boys sliding down the staircase.

Mostly, Mr. Godfrey hoped that he would not run into Mrs. Koch for the rest of the evening. Thus, he decided to stay in his quarters for the remainder of the night. *I hope those boys stay out of trouble.*

Mr. Godfrey thought back to the last time Mrs. Koch got upset with him. She went on for hours, shouting at the top of her lungs. She repeated the same thing over and over and over again. Mr. Godfrey shook his head. *Please, not tonight.*

The doorknob clicked as Mr. Godfrey tilted his head and entered the front door. He listened for the whereabouts of Mrs. Koch. All that was heard was silence. Relief could be seen on his face as he pushed the door open.

The house was silent. Mr. Godfrey walked across the floor and looked up at the staircase. When he turned back around, Mrs. Koch was staring directly at him from across the foyer. Her arms were crossed. "HUMPH, Just my luck," Mr. Godfrey sighed.

❖ ❖ ❖

Mrs. Koch's voice could be heard all the way in Clara's room, drowning out the screeching – scratching - skittering noise coming from Clara's closet.

Clara looked back at her bed as she dashed out of her room. She ran down the hallway toward the grand staircase. She passed Fritz's bedroom. His door was now open. She didn't see him or Bruno. She hoped that nothing had happened to them.

Clara reached the staircase as fast as she could. She looked over the banister and saw Mrs. Koch and Mr. Godfrey. Mrs. Koch stared at Clara with a startled look. Mr. Godfrey looked with alarm. Clara's hair was disheveled as she ran down the stairs.

"Egon!" Clara screamed as she pointed toward the top of the stairs.

At the same time, in unison, Mr. Godfrey and Mrs. Koch turned their heads and looked in the direction that Clara was pointing.

"Egon?" Mrs. Koch said, as if not understanding.

"Egon is in my bedroom. He's in my closet!" Clara exclaimed. "I heard it again, just like last time, on Christmas Eve!" Clara panted, out of breath. Her whole body shook as she pointed to the top of the staircase.

Mrs. Koch and Mr. Godfrey looked at Clara, then stared at each other with puzzled faces.

"Clara, are you saying that, that creature from the Black Forest, is upstairs in your bedroom?" Mrs. Koch asked in a worried tone.

Clara shook her head rapidly. She remembered that when she had returned from the Black Forest, last Christmas, she told everyone about her adventure, but nobody believed her story.

They did not believe that her Nutcracker Soldier doll that she received as a gift from her Uncle Drosselmeyer, was indeed a *real* prince, Prince Dustin.

They did not believe that her Uncle Drosselmeyer had turned Prince Dustin into a doll. Nor did they believe that her Uncle Drosselmeyer was actually a wizard.

They did not believe that Prince Dustin slew the Mouse King, in their parlor. They also did not believe that there was an Egon, who was the Mouse King's brother.

And they surely did not believe that Clara had traveled *deep in the Black Forest*.

An image of Egon shot through Clara's mind. Egon was big, as tall as Clara's father.

He looked like a human-sized rat. He had pointed teeth that dripped with drool from constant gnawing. His belly protruded as if it were stuffed. His eyes, a frightful black, never blinked.

Mr. Godfrey saw the fear on Clara's face. Maybe now believing her story, he raced up the staircase with a wild look. Clara followed behind Mr. Godfrey. Mrs. Koch followed behind Clara. They got to the top of the stairs and then charged down the hall. Passing Fritz's bedroom, Clara peeped inside. Her face dropped, she did not see Fritz or Bruno. *Oh, no, I hope they are safe!*

Mr. Godfrey stopped outside of Clara's bedroom. He looked back at Clara and Mrs. Koch. He waved at them to stay back. Clara ignored him and ran to Mr. Godfrey's side.

"No, no, Clara. Get back," Mr. Godfrey said, peering inside Clara's bedroom. Mr. Godfrey stood ready to attack the creature that was after Clara. They all stood in silence. Nobody uttered a word. Their heads were tilted, listening.

A screeching – scratching - skittering sound was coming from Clara's closet.

Mr. Godfrey charged into Clara's bedroom.

❖ ❖ ❖

This can't be happening. Clara wiped the sweat off her forehead. Clara thought back to Christmas Eve. The grandfather clock in the grand parlor had struck the midnight hour. Clara recounted walking down the hallway. She heard eerie sounds coming from the parlor: screeching - scratching - skittering sounds.

Clara didn't want to think back to all that happened that night. Clara wanted to forget. She wanted to forget about the giant mice that were in her parlor last Christmas Eve. She wanted to forget about the creatures in the Black Forest. She wanted to forget about being ripped out their small boat and tossed down the waterfall. Mostly, Clara wanted to forget about Egon.

She only wanted to remember Prince Dustin and Princess Sugar Plum, Queen Nordika, Bronson and the General, the Land of Sweets and the Ice Palace in the Land of Snow.

However, the horrid images of Egon, standing on his hind legs, gnawing and gnawing, took over her mind. She could almost smell the stench coming from his body. *He smelled like rotten meat,* she recounted. Clara recalled Prince Dustin saying that Egon would come after her for revenge. "You are not safe as long as Egon is alive."

Clara shook. "Egon is here!"

-4-

The Note

The old man dressed in all black crept across the stone floor in a room in the cellar of the Log Cabin Castle. With hunched shoulders, he looked like a shadow unattached from a body. His black cape seemed to pull his body down. The pounding of his feet echoed off the walls. His steps sounded heavy, making him appear to have more strength than his appearance indicated.

He looked neither to the right, nor to the left, but straight ahead. He seemed to be heading toward the opposite side of the room, toward a door. The door seemed to be made of metal and timber. It looked like it led outside. A brass plate with a keyhole was beneath the door's lever.

Pointed fingernails protruded from the man's skinny fingers as he lifted the door's lever. The door was locked from the inside. The creepy man knocked on the door.

KNOCK-KNOCK   KNOCK-KNOCK

The man cocked his head underneath his rumpled top hat. Not hearing anything from the other side, he knocked again.

KNOCK-KNOCK   KNOCK-KNOCK

The man stood still and listened. A sly grin erupted on his face when he heard a loud knocking from the other side of the door.

KNOCK   KNOCK   KNOCK

With his fingers fumbling, he reached into his pants pocket and pulled out a brass skeleton key. He jabbed the key into the keyhole. He paused after hearing a clicking sound. He then stepped back and watched. The door's lever turned and slowly the door opened. The man in all black nodded, as if saluting. *It* entered.

❖ ❖ ❖

Prince Dustin heard the orchestra playing as he buttoned the jacket to his formal blue and red uniform. The jacket was adorned with gold cords, bands, and buttons. Looking at his reflection in the mirror, he thought, *I wish my parents were here.* Although he felt honored to be crowned King of Konfetenburg, Prince Dustin missed his parents.

When activities settle down, we will go deeper into the Black Forest and search for them again, he resolved privately. Although he and Princess Sugar Plum looked throughout the Black Forest for their parents, they were advised not to venture into the deepest parts of the forest, without the full escort of Konfetenburg's army.

Prince Dustin thought about the Kreaturs that lived deeper in the forest. He remembered being told, "You cannot outrun them. You cannot outfight them. You will not survive them." With a determined look, he said silently, *I will be the first. If my parents are there, I will bring them back.*

"Prince Dustin, they are ready for you in the Grand Hall," Bronson, the beaver, said. Prince Dustin and Bronson had become great friends ever since their time in the Black Forest last Christmas Eve.

Generations ago, deep in the Black Forest, many of the animals and humans learned to communicate and talk with each other, without either group having to change their language.

Standing on his hind legs, Bronson was as tall as Prince Dustin. As are most of the animals deep in the Black Forest, Bronson was much larger than other beavers.

Bronson's chocolate brown, thick fur coat had been brushed until it shined like mink. When the attendants tried to file his nails for the event, he refused, with a grunt. Bronson was the leader of the beaver scouts that lived with the other beavers along the Stromabwarts River.

"Thank you, Bronson," Prince Dustin said. "I am almost ready." Prince Dustin took one last look at his reflection in the mirror. He pulled at the bottom of his jacket, although it didn't need to be straightened, it had not a wrinkle. His shoulder-length light brown hair was curled slightly at the back of his neck. His sapphire eyes complemented his blue and red uniform.

Prince Dustin grasped the handle of his sword. It hung in a sheath by his side. With a look of confidence on his face, Prince Dustin said, "I am ready." The tight grip of his hand on his sword may have revealed otherwise.

Bronson nodded with encouragement, as if he understood. Prince Dustin was really saying that he was ready to assume the duties of King of Konfetenburg.

❖ ❖ ❖

It entered the cellar of the Log Cabin Castle. The creature's massive body took up the entire threshold of the door. His intimidating presence was undeniable. As the creature moved closer to the old man in all black, the man lowered his head and seemed to hold his breath, as if trying to avoid the smell coming from the beast.

The creature snarled, "Nordika thought that she could keep me locked up in that dungeon." The beast spat sharply on the chamber's floor. "They have yet to see my fury!" The creature cracked its knuckles. The noise sounded like bones breaking.

The beast's eyes were the blackest of black, and rimmed in red. Its rough fur coat was filthy-gray. It's cone sharp muzzle resembled that of a rat. His tail was long, ringed and scaly. His tail whipped the air, making a snapping sound.

Seeing the creature, the creepy man bowed. Holding the edge of his black cape in one hand and tipping his rumpled black hat with the other, he said. "Your Highness, I look forward to our new alliance." The old man laughed. His laughter sounded like pure evil.

The beast hissed. "And what is the plan, Drosselmeyer?"

Drosselmeyer furrowed his brows and narrowed his eyes. "It is time for sweet revenge."

❖ ❖ ❖

The trumpets signaled that the coronation of Prince Dustin Egbert Conrad von Konig to King of Konfetenburg had commenced. No detail was spared, the Grand Hall of the Log Cabin Castle was decorated with wreaths and flowers from across the lands.

Prince Dustin could hear the orchestra as he walked toward the Grand Hall. The foyer was clear of guests, but bustling with attendants, carrying trays of sweets and treats: chocolate lebkuchen cookies, plum tarts, raspberry custard in cups, and other delectable goodies. The servants bowed as they passed Prince Dustin.

Prince Dustin nodded at the attendants as he walked. He held his head high. Excitement from all the dignitaries and guests was louder the closer he got to the entrance of the hall.

Attendants on each side of the doors opened them slowly, bowing with obvious pleasure.

When the doors were opened entirely, Prince Dustin stepped inside the room and stood at the entrance. Everyone applauded. It almost sounded like thunder. The conductor of the orchestra raised his baton higher, and the orchestra transitioned to the *March of Konfetenburg*. Prince Dustin marched into the room, in rhythm with the robust and steady percussion sound of the music.

The assembly erupted as Prince Dustin stepped across the floor. Vibrant garments and gowns in orange and red, to blue and gold, lined the chamber. Everyone wore wide smiles and bright eyes, like jewelry.

Prince Dustin commanded the attention of everyone. He made eye contact with all the dignitaries and many guests from all the nearby kingdoms in the Black Forest. Prince Dustin had observed his father, King Marc, many times.

Prince Dustin marched across the floor displaying confidence. Nobody seemed to notice that he was gripping the handle of his sword so tightly that the palm of his hand dripped sweat.

Prince Dustin reached a decorated stage that held a jewel-embellished red velvet throne. With a nod and a wave, Prince Dustin acknowledged the crowd before taking his seat. The Grand Hall darkened, and a hush filled the room.

A crystal spotlight illuminated the orchestra. The orchestra began playing a soft selection. Flutes, clarinets, and violins were prominent in this musical score. Whispers could be heard from the crowd:

"Princess Sugar Plum will be performing!"
"She is such a beautiful dancer."

"I love watching her spin and twirl."
"This is going to be such a treat."
"It's like she floats on air!"

Every eye in the room looked at the entrance of the Grand Hall. Princess Sugar Plum did not appear. The orchestra repeated the beginning of the selection. Still, Princess Sugar Plum did not appear. The whispers continued:

"Where is Princess Sugar Plum?"
"I have not seen her all afternoon."
"Where could she be?"

Princess Sugar Plum still did not appear. The conductor of the orchestra looked across the room and raised his baton to repeat the beginning of the selection for the third time.

Prince Dustin stood. Worry could be seen across his face. Queen Nordika then stood and said something to the General. The General charged out of the Grand Hall, running on all four legs. His ears were pricked and his fangs exposed. All the guests backed away as he raced past them.

Prince Dustin held the handle of his sword as he hurried out of the Grand Hall. Bronson and Queen Nordika followed Prince Dustin. All the guests stared with wide eyes and open mouths. The music stopped abruptly.

Gertrude announced to the guests, "Everyone! Princess Sugar Plum is probably on her way down. Please help yourselves to more sweets." Gertrude signaled the orchestra to continue with another selection. Servers entered the room with trays of sweets and treats. The orchestra played a different selection. The piece had a slow beat, building up to a crescendo that never came.

❖ ❖ ❖

The General was the first to make it to Princess Sugar Plum's bedroom chamber. He seemed to smell something in the air. He jerked his head from side to side, sniffing the air. He then howled like a wolf.

"Sugar Plum! Sugar Plum!" Prince Dustin shouted. He bolted into her bedroom chamber. His eyes were red, but his face looked fierce.

Queen Nordika entered Princess Sugar Plum's bedroom chamber after Prince Dustin. She scanned the room, as if she were assessing the situation. The General moved toward Queen Nordika. He must have communicated something dire because Queen Nordika's face went stiff. Prince Dustin looked as though he overheard the General. Without hesitation, he ran into the adjoining room.

Bronson followed. He sniffed the floor as he alternated between walking on his two hind legs and all four. Queen Nordika and the General joined Prince Dustin and Bronson in the connecting room.

"She's not here!" Prince Dustin darted over to Princess Sugar Plum's dresser bureau. A torn note was left on top of the dresser. Next to the note, Prince Dustin saw a black eye patch. Prince Dustin picked up the eye patch, "Herr Drosselmeyer?" Prince Dustin said in a questioning tone.

"It's worse than that," Queen Nordika said gravely. "It's Egon. Egon must have escaped. Egon was here. The General smelled his scent." The General nodded confirmation.

Prince Dustin read the note aloud:

Dusty,

By the time you find this note, it will be too late. We have taken the little fairy princess to the dungeon at Niedertrachtig Castle, deeper in the Black Forest. We will exchange the little fairy for the little girl, Clara. Clara will have to pay the price for her part in the death of my brother. And don't think I forgot about you, Dusty!

You have 3 days to bring Clara to us at Niedertrachtig Castle or say goodbye to the little fairy princess.

P.S. Drosselmeyer left something for you.

Signed: King Egon

"Egon did escape!" Prince Dustin shook his head wildly in disbelief. He continued,

"Herr Drosselmeyer and Egon, they are working together." Prince Dustin lowered his eyes. "It is my fault." Prince Dustin stared at the floor as he continued, "They kidnapped Princess Sugar Plum."

- 5 -

Screeching – Scratching – Skittering

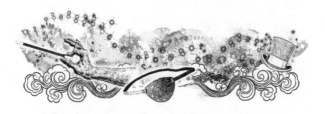

Clara gasped. Her head was cocked as she stood inside her bedroom. "Did you hear that?" she whispered to Mr. Godfrey.

Screeching - scratching - skittering sounds were coming from Clara's closet!

Mr. Godfrey's face sunk and his cheeks hollowed. "Something *is* in your closet," he confirmed. Sweat dripped down Mr. Godfrey's forehead. His head jerked as he looked around the room with bulging eyes.

Clara panted as she glared out her bedroom window. She hoped that Prince Dustin and his soldiers would appear, like last Christmas Eve. They did not.

The sounds from the closet got even louder. "Get back, Clara! Get back!" Mr. Godfrey yelled. He turned and looked over at the fireplace in Clara's room. "That will work," he said as he rushed over and grabbed the fireplace poker off the stand. With both hands, Mr. Godfrey squeezed the handle of the poker. He held it above his head and slowly stepped toward Clara's closet.

Clara bolted toward the fireplace. She grabbed the fireplace shovel off the stand and held it high. She glanced at Mr. Godfrey, without looking into his eyes. *I am not going to let Egon hurt you or Mrs. Koch,* Clara said silently.

Mr. Godfrey frowned at Clara, as he waved at her to stay back.

Clara remembered Queen Nordika telling her, "You were very brave. If it were not for you, we don't know what might have happened." *Be brave. Be brave. Be brave.* Clara chanted quietly. Her hands trembled as she clung to the fireplace shovel. The shovel kept slipping from the sweat on her palms. She continued to chant with determination, *Be brave.*

"Get back, Clara. It's coming after you!" Mrs. Koch screamed. Clara jerked.

Mr. Godfrey rushed to the closet door. He glanced over his shoulder at Clara with worried eyes.

Mrs. Koch ran toward Clara. She grabbed Clara and held her tightly in her arms. Clara could not move. The vessels in Mrs. Koch's neck pulsated, and she made a wheezing sound as her chest pumped up and down. Clara could barely breathe. Mr. Godfrey nodded approvingly at Mrs. Koch for keeping Clara away from the closet.

With a tense look on his face, Mr. Godfrey turned toward the closet. The screeching - scratching - skittering sounds got louder. Holding the fireplace poker with his left hand, Mr. Godfrey grabbed the doorknob of the closet with his other hand. He stood back as he turned the knob. The door c-r-e-a-k-e-d.

Mr. Godfrey shifted his weight and gripped the poker tighter and higher. The noise from the closet stopped. In the background, the distant sound of boys playing stickball outside could be heard. Clara glanced over at her bedroom window. She thought about Fritz. Clara hoped that he and Bruno were outside, safe, playing stickball.

Mr. Godfrey lunged and pulled the closet door wide open. He stood ready. Mrs. Koch looked at the open door with a fixed stare. Clara could see inside her closet. Her clothes were neatly hung, but her shoes were scattered on the floor inside the closet. She stared. *Where is Egon?*

Clara continued to listen but still did not hear the screeching - scratching - skittering sounds that had come from her closet just moments before. *Where is Egon?* she continued to wonder. All remained quiet with fixed eyes.

THEN—something was heard rustling from the back of Clara's closet. Mr. Godfrey lifted the poker above his head and stood ready. Mrs. Koch tried to pull Clara back.

Clara managed to wriggle free and held her shovel over her head like a baseball bat. "I am not going to let Egon hurt you, Mrs. Koch," Clara said, not taking her eyes off the closet.

Mr. Godfrey raised the fireplace poker above his head. Mrs. Koch shrieked with horror. Clara stood steady.

"Get back, Clara," Mr. Godfrey repeated, in a firmer voice, this time. Clara did not move back. She raised the shovel even higher.

The creatures in the closet rushed out in a flurry! Mr. Godfrey stared at the creatures. Mrs. Koch looked to be in shock. Clara blinked.

Fritz and Bruno laughed wildly, jumping up and down as they vaulted out of Clara's closet. Their heads bobbed and they held their stomachs. Fritz bowled over with laughter as he pointed to the expression on Mrs. Koch's face.

Fritz and Bruno were out of control with laughter. Fritz raised a toy in his hand and rolled it across the door of the closet. It made a screeching - scratching - skittering sound.

"Fooled you, Clara!" Fritz hooted with genuine satisfaction.

Nobody laughed, not Clara, Mr. Godfrey nor Mrs. Koch. Their faces displayed quite the opposite expression. Looking at their faces, Fritz swallowed. Bruno looked away. Fritz then glanced up at them with *that innocent look.*

❖ ❖ ❖

Later in the afternoon, alone in her bedroom, Clara was still upset at Fritz and even more excited, about spending the rest of the week over Marie's house. Clara remembered that she still needed to pack her hairbrush and ribbons. She was able to squeeze her ribbons and hairbrush in her luggage.

Clara looked at her Nutcracker Soldier doll. It was back on top of her pillow. Clara was glad that Fritz hadn't broken it like he did on Christmas Eve.

Clara had changed her clothes and was wearing a simple blue apron dress with soft, white balloon sleeves. The dress flared out with lightweight crinoline and tied in the back at the waist. It hit just below her knee. Clara arched her right foot. She had decided to wear her toe shoes and white ruffled pantaloons. *Since we'll mostly be dancing,* she reasoned.

Clara stepped over to her bureau and looked into the mirror. Using blue ribbons, she pulled her spiral curls into two ponytails. The chestnut ponytails bounced when she walked. "Argh, Mother does a better job," Clara sighed, looking at the uneven ribbons.

Although it had not rained, the sky remained overcast. Clara thought about the prank that Fritz played on her earlier. Fritz and Bruno were sent to Fritz's bedroom for the rest of the evening. Clara wondered what they were doing.

Clara could still hear some of the boys playing outside. She went over to her window to watch. She saw a handful of the older boys. She recognized all of them. She saw the older Brecht boys. Clara frowned. They always teased Clara and her friends.

C-R-E-A-K

Clara's bedroom door creaked open. Clara was still jittery from Fritz's practical joke. Hearing the creaking sound of her bedroom door, Clara turned around quickly, "Fritz, you were supposed to stay—"

Clara's jaw dropped before she could finish her sentence. Clara stood still with her eyes wide and mouth open. Prince Dustin, the General, and Bronson were standing just inside her bedroom.

With her arms behind her, Clara held tight to the windowsill. She stared with disbelief. *This cannot be real.*

Prince Dustin was standing next to Clara's dresser. Clara was stunned. She never thought she would see Prince Dustin again. Yet, here he was. After Clara was over her initial surprise of seeing Prince Dustin, she immediately noticed that he looked worried. *Something is wrong,* she thought. "Prince Dustin?" she said in a questioning tone.

"Hello Clara," Prince Dustin responded, pulling at the bottom of his blue and red jacket. Bronson and the General stood next to Prince Dustin. They had apparently snuck into the Stahlbaum's home, probably flew in through an open window, without being seen. The General barked, communicating something to Prince Dustin. Prince Dustin nodded. Clara winced, not understanding what the shepherd communicated.

Prince Dustin said with a severe look, "We are sorry to have to get you involved." Clara parted her lips. She could tell that something was seriously wrong. "Egon and Herr Dross—," Prince Dustin's voice trailed off. He exchanged glances with Bronson and the General before continuing. "Egon escaped from the Ice Palace," Prince Dustin continued.

"Oh no!" Clara shrieked, covering her mouth with her hand.

"Queen Nordika said he had help escaping." Prince Dustin stared glumly at Clara.

"He didn't hurt Queen Nordika, did he?" Clara asked with alarm. The General barked softly. Clara did not know what the General was communicating, but the way he barked encouraged her that Queen Nordika was not hurt.

"Queen Nordika is well," Prince Dustin said, looking away.

Clara breathed a sigh of relief. She was glad that Queen Nordika was safe. She then grimaced. Clara's eyes gazed at each of them. Someone was missing.

"And Princess Sugar Plum?" Clara said in a soft voice.

Prince Dustin shook his head. He then looked directly into Clara's eyes. "Egon kidnapped Sugar Plum."

Clara gasped! Her eyelids closed, and her legs fell from underneath her as she passed out. Prince Dustin ran over and caught Clara before she hit the floor. He and Bronson laid Clara gently on her bed.

The General quickly picked up the Nutcracker Soldier doll off the bed pillow with his mouth, to get it out the way. He released the doll on the chair next to Clara's bed.

Prince Dustin stood on the left side of Clara's bed. Bronson and the General stood at the foot. All were quiet.

❖ ❖ ❖

Clara rubbed her eyes as she awoke. She slowly looked over at her Nutcracker Soldier doll resting on her chair. *That was a bad dream,* she thought. *I wonder what time it is, Marie will be here soon.*

"Clara," Prince Dustin said softly, "Are you okay?"

Clara sprung up and turned her head toward the sound of Prince Dustin's voice. "Prince Dustin? You really are here," Clara said. Clara looked at Prince Dustin with troubled eyes. "That wasn't a dream? Egon kidnapped Princess Sugar Plum?"

Prince Dustin nodded.

"Egon has Princess Sugar Plum?" Clara asked again, as if she wanted a different answer.

"Yes." Prince Dustin went on to explain how Egon escaped from the Ice Palace. He told Clara that Egon kidnapped Sugar Plum right before he was to be crowned King of Konfetenburg.

Prince Dustin did not mention Herr Drosselmeyer's part in the kidnapping, probably thinking that it would be too much for Clara, all at once.

"Everyone was in the Grand Hall waiting for Princess Sugar Plum to dance. The orchestra kept replaying the introduction of her music," Prince Dustin said. His voice gradually got lower as he recounted what happened.

Bronson grunted.

Prince Dustin continued, "When we made it up to Sugar Plum's chambers, the General could smell that Egon had been there."

Clara quivered. Her eyes were puffy, and her cheeks flushed.

"Egon left a note," Prince Dustin said. Prince Dustin then handed the note to Clara.

Clara held the note and began reading it in earnest. She wiped the sweat off her forehead. Her eyes jetted from left to right, as she read the note. Clara's face visibly changed color. She continued reading. Her face went from red to pink to its natural tone. Even her eyes cleared.

After reading the note, Clara leaped off the bed. She looked at Prince Dustin with dry eyes. "We have three days."

Prince Dustin smiled without showing his teeth, probably trying to display more confidence than he actually felt. "I have a plan."

Clara nodded with eager eyes as she listened to the plan.

The rustling sound continued as more Knuddeligs came out from behind the trees.

ACT 2

-6-

The Thing

The skies got darker the deeper they traveled into the Black Forest. It was late evening. The clouds seemed to vanish, little by little. It was as though the clouds were being eaten up by the sky, piece by piece.

"You don't have your eyes closed this time, Clara?" Prince Dustin said in a questioning tone. "The last time when we flew, you had your eyes closed the entire time."

"Uhm, we're not going to fall, right?"

Prince Dustin gripped Clara's hand even tighter. "I promise, Clara. We will not fall." He glanced over at Bronson and the

General before continuing, "My energy force is keeping everybody in the sky."

Prince Dustin added, "When Princess Sugar Plum asked the Great Tree to grant me the ability to fly like the Tree Fairies, the Great Tree created a great energy force around me. Anyone inside my energy field will be pulled toward my energy, and not fall."

"Bronson and the General too?" Clara asked, with a hint of worry. She noticed that they were not linking hands with Prince Dustin.

Prince Dustin nodded. "Would you like for me to let go of your hand now, Clara? You won't fall."

Clara shook her head quickly. Prince Dustin grinned.

Clara looked down at the forest below. Darkness had not yet fully consumed the evening. Tall, emerald-green spruce and fir trees covered the land. Clara thought that the trees looked even more beautiful this time, without their white, winter coats.

Clara felt her body glide smoothly through the sky. Her heart raced. Her body didn't seem to have any weight at all. It reminded Clara of times when she went swimming in the lake near her Uncle Drosselmeyer's old mill. Sometimes, she would float in the water and look up at the blue sky.

Flying is like floating in deep water, Clara thought.

An eagle soared below. Clara noticed that the eagle was not flapping its wings. The eagle would dip down, and then rise as if it were riding a wave. *I wish I could soar like eagles.* Clara beamed as she loosened her grip on Prince Dustin's hand.

"Are you more comfortable now, Clara?" Prince Dustin asked.

Clara nodded as she let loose of Prince Dustin's hand. "I am now flying like that eagle," Clara said, stretching out her arms.

❖ ❖ ❖

After some time, stars gradually appeared. A galaxy of stars now twinkled, illuminating the black-velvet night. Clara could no longer see the trees. The forest below looked like a black abyss, without a beginning or an end.

Clara's heart pounded. She could feel herself breathing as she stared into the pit of darkness below. She glanced over at Prince Dustin and hoped he did not sense her fear. *I am brave. I am brave. I am brave,* Clara repeated silently to herself. She tried to avoid looking down.

"Do you think they will check for you," Prince Dustin said, "at your friend's house?"

Clara recalled the events that had happened earlier in the evening before responding.

❖ ❖ ❖

Clara had managed to elude Mrs. Koch and Mr. Godfrey. Mrs. Koch was busy in the kitchen, and Mr. Godfrey was in his room for the night, avoiding Mrs. Koch.

Clara had told Mrs. Koch, she was leaving and answered the door when Marie's mother and Marie arrived. Clara had explained to Marie that she did not feel well. Clara coughed like Fritz did when he tried to stay home from school.

"Be sure to have Mrs. Koch bake you some zwieback. It will make you feel better," Marie's mother had said.

Marie gave Clara a gentle hug before departing. "I hope you feel better soon, Clara."

Clara then tiptoed back up the grand staircase. Fritz's bedroom door was still closed. Clara hid her luggage inside her closet. Prince Dustin, Clara, Bronson, and the General then leaped out of Clara's bedroom window to rescue Princess Sugar Plum, Clara recounted.

❖ ❖ ❖

Clara was quiet thinking about the earlier events in her mind. Not hearing a response from Clara, Prince Dustin repeated his question, "Do you think they will check for you at your friend's house?"

"I'm sorry, I was just thinking. They will be so busy keeping up with Fritz and Bruno they won't have time to check on me." Prince Dustin chuckled.

As they continued to fly, everyone remained quiet for a while, as if each of them were in deep thought.

"We will be landing soon, Clara. We are now *deeper* in the Black Forest." Prince Dustin gripped the handle of his sword and looked down into the black forest.

Clara nodded in slow motion. She noticed a hint of caution in Prince Dustin's voice.

With her eyes narrowed, Clara looked at Bronson and the General. They seemed focused on their thoughts. She wasn't sure if they had heard Prince Dustin.

Clara thought back to Christmas Eve. She recalled Prince Dustin telling her about places deeper in the Black Forest. "There are places even deeper in the Black Forest than my kingdom. The Black Forest has places that are very dangerous," she remembered Prince Dustin telling her last time. He also told her that he had never traveled to those dangerous places.

Clara shivered. She tried not to look down. The more she thought about places deeper in the Black Forest, the more frightened she got, the more frightened she got, the more she looked down. The General barked softly looking over at Clara. He probably sensed her fear.

"Clara, we aren't going to fall," Prince Dustin said in a concerned tone.

Clara hoped her face was not flushed.

"We are going to be on the ground soon. We have actually been descending," Prince Dustin continued.

Clara tried to smile. She was no longer afraid of flying—she was afraid of landing—deeper in the Black Forest. Clara swallowed as she looked down. *Nothing seems to be moving.* Clara shrugged. *Something's waiting for us down there.* Clara repeated to herself, *I am brave. I am brave. I am brave.*

Prince Dustin communicated with Bronson and the General. The three conversed continuously for the remainder of their descent. Clara was able to understand Prince Dustin, but only heard grunts and barks as Bronson and the General communicated.

Clara noticed that they would glance in her direction, probably forgetting that she was not able to understand. She was not from deep in Black Forest where people and animals had learned to communicate with each other centuries ago.

Clara responded with a smile. She was glad to be part of the team, even though she had no idea what the team was communicating.

After a short time, Prince Dustin looked over at Clara. "We are going to rest there, Clara," Prince Dustin said, pointing to a clearing between the trees, at the edge of the river.

Clara nodded as she looked down at the barren spot. She thought it looked like the river they had journeyed down last Christmas Eve. However, something felt different about this river, she thought. Although the river looked tranquil, Clara sensed danger. She felt a chill go down her back.

They landed smoothly. Clara felt her body move forward, but she was able to maintain her balance when her feet touched the ground.

Clara was unable to make out the shapes of anything in the forest. *Everything looks scary and black,* Clara thought. Yes, they were deeper in the Black Forest. "A place where few rarely returned," Clara recalled Prince Dustin saying last Christmas Eve.

"There's a soft bed of grass," Prince Dustin said, pointing. "You can sleep there, Clara. We will set out at sunrise."

I don't really need to sleep, Clara thought, looking around. She didn't want to close her eyes for a second.

"Okay," Clara responded. She settled on the grassy patch. *It is soft,* Clara thought. She smiled as she looked up at the stars.

Although she could not see any flowers close by, Clara thought she smelled the scent of lavender. It reminded her of her mother. Mrs. Stahlbaum always wore lavender-scented perfume. Clara started to relax, as she stretched out on the soft grass.

Before closing her eyes, Clara saw the others sitting near the river just a few feet away. Prince Dustin whispered while Bronson grunted softly. At times, Prince Dustin would glance over at Clara, as if making sure she was okay.

The General seemed focused and was looking around with his eyes narrowed and his ears perked. He remained quiet and attentive, Clara observed. After watching them for a few minutes, Clara was overcome by the relaxing sound of the river flowing downstream. She closed her eyes and drifted off into a deep sleep.

❖ ❖ ❖

After some time, Clara woke suddenly! She heard sounds coming from the forest. She noticed that all the stars had disappeared. Clara's eyes widened. The sound of heavy footsteps was coming from the forest. Clara trembled. Whatever it was, it was moving closer. Clara heard the cracking sound of twigs and branches breaking. It was moving in her direction, straight toward Clara.

Where's Prince Dustin? Clara panicked. She looked around but did not see Prince Dustin, Bronson or the General.

Where did they go? Clara couldn't imagine them leaving her alone. *That Thing in the trees must have taken them!* Clara's face turned bright red with worry.

Thump-Thump	*Thump-Thump*
Thump-Thump	*Thump-Thump*
Thump-Thump	*Thump-Thump*

Clara crouched down in the tall grass. The thumping sound of The Thing in the forest was getting closer. Clara peeped through the needles of the grass. She only saw darkness.

THUMP-THUMP	***THUMP-THUMP***
THUMP-THUMP	***THUMP-THUMP***
THUMP-THUMP	***THUMP-THUMP***

I can't stay here! If it gets me, then I won't be able to help Prince Dustin or Bronson or the General, Clara thought.

Clara looked at the tall trees on the other side of the clearing and reasoned, *If I can make it to the trees on the other side, then I can hide in the forest. Then I can look for the others. They may need me.*

Clara's heart raced, and sweat dripped from her forehead. She tried not to breathe loud. *I hope that Thing doesn't hear me,* she thought.

Clara looked back into the trees. She then shot up and ran as fast as she could. She ran without looking back. She just kept running. She was almost at the trees on the other side. *I'm almost there! Just a little further.*

Clara was near a huge tree. It was just a few feet ahead.

I can hide behind that tree until that Thing is gone. Then I can figure out how to rescue Prince Dustin, Bronson, and the General. However—it was too late.

The Thing grabbed Clara.

-7-

Magical Crystal Stone Necklace

THE THING grabbed Clara's shoulder and shook her. Clara was face down, on the grass. She thrashed her arms and legs into the ground, fighting to get free. She scratched at the ground so deeply that dirt got underneath her fingernails. Clara knew she had to break free so that she could somehow save the others. She continued to wrestle. *I can't let it take me.*

The Thing continued to shake Clara. Clara's shoulder throbbed in pain. Clara did not stop, she continued to wrestle, trying to wriggle loose.

"CLARA!"

Clara stopped writhing and twisting her body. *That Thing knows my name? Egon must have sent it to capture me,* Clara thought.

"Clara! Wake up—Clara!" Prince Dustin said, shaking Clara's shoulder. Bronson and the General looked on, staring at Clara.

Prince Dustin? Clara thought she heard Prince Dustin's voice. *Now I'm hearing things,* Clara thought.

"Clara, you are having a bad dream. Wake up." Prince Dustin stopped shaking Clara's shoulder. "Clara, it's me. It's me, Prince Dustin. You must have had a bad dream."

Clara's heart pounded in her chest. "Prince Dustin?" Clara sat up slowly and looked at Prince Dustin with a quizzical look. "Was I dreaming? Was that a dr—dream?" Clara said softly, beginning to comprehend.

Prince Dustin nodded with gentle eyes.

Clara's heart was still beating fast. She looked down at her hands. Her palms were covered with blades of grass. Sweat had glued the grass to her hands. Clara started to pull the grass off her hands.

Prince Dustin said softly, "You might want to start with your face." Bits of chopped-off grass covered Clara's face. Bronson grunted several times and the General barked. Clara laughed. She did not want them to know how silly she actually felt. *It was just a dream.* She was partly relieved, mostly embarrassed.

Clara washed her face and hands in the river. She heard Prince Dustin talking to Bronson and the General. The sky was no longer black, the stars were no longer shining, and the moon had disappeared. However, the sun had not yet awakened.

It must be early in the morning, Clara thought. She looked at her reflection in the river. Her face was clean. Clara sighed silently, *I wish I were brave like Queen Nordika.*

Food could be smelled in the air. Clara turned and sniffed. Bronson had caught fish from the river, and Prince Dustin was grilling the fish over a flame. Clara leaped to her feet as she remembered that they had three days to get to Princess Sugar Plum and this was the beginning of Day Two.

❖ ❖ ❖

Prince Dustin, Clara, Bronson, and the General had been walking through the forest for a while. The sun now peeked through crevices of the dense pine trees, like water trickling through cracks in a roof.

Bouquets of wildflowers in every color of the rainbow covered the ground. When Clara stepped through patches of flowers, an intense burst of the flower's fragrance filled the air.

Clara heard small animals in the distance. It sounded like the animals were playing. *So far, 'deeper in the Black Forest' seems like a beautiful place*, Clara thought.

Clara looked ahead. Prince Dustin and Bronson were leading them deeper into the forest. They were communicating something. Clara wondered what they were talking about. *I wish I could talk to the animals like Prince Dustin.*

Clara quickly glanced behind her at the General. He seemed to be neither smiling nor frowning. His ears were perked, and his tail was held high. Clara noticed that his eyes were moving from side to side, as if he were scanning the area.

Clara wondered what the General heard that she could not hear. What did he see that could not see. She glared at the dense pine trees that were all around. *What do you see, General?*

"We're going to stop ahead," Prince Dustin said, looking back at Clara. "We'll rest for a few minutes."

Clara was glad that they were about to stop. A rock had gotten lodged in her shoe, and she wanted to remove it. Clara felt it each time she stepped. She hadn't wanted to ask them to stop just to take a rock out of her shoe.

Prince Dustin, Bronson and Clara plopped down underneath a tall tree. The tree was so large that each of them could rest their backs against the same side of the tree. The General stood. Clara noticed that his eyes were still moving from side to side and his ears were pricked.

Clara pulled off her dance slipper and took the rock out. She pulled the cords on her shoes tighter so that no more rocks could get lodged in her shoes. She noticed that the rock, although much smaller and not as shiny, reminded her of the crystal stone necklace that Prince Dustin had given her last Christmas Eve.

"This crystal will keep you warm deep in the Black Forest," Prince Dustin had said. *It did keep me warm,* Clara recounted. She kept the necklace tucked underneath her clothes, never taking it off. Clara pulled the necklace out from the top of her dress. The crystal stone glowed.

"You wore the necklace, Clara?" Prince Dustin said with surprise.

"I wear it all the time. I keep it tucked underneath my clothes." Clara smiled.

Prince Dustin seemed pleased that Clara was wearing the necklace. "The crystal stone can do many things. You might need it," he said.

Clara held the crystal stone to her eyes and wondered. *What else can it do?* She then tucked the necklace back underneath the top of her dress.

"Are you ready, Clara? We still have a long journey ahead of us." Prince Dustin gripped the handle of his sword as he stood.

"Yes," Clara said, springing up.

"Would you like to walk in the front with me, Clara? I have something I really need to tell you." Prince Dustin had not yet told Clara about her Uncle Drosselmeyer's involvement with kidnapping Princess Sugar Plum.

Clara walked alongside Prince Dustin. Bronson followed closely behind them. The General followed behind Bronson. Clara figured that the General was always on guard. She was glad that Queen Nordika had the General join them on their journey.

Clara wondered how much longer it would take before they got to the castle where Princess Sugar Plum was being held captive. She thought about Egon and the stench of doom funneling, like black smoke, out of his nostrils.

Although the thought of Egon still frightened Clara, she did not shiver thinking about him this time. *We must save Princess Sugar Plum,* she thought with a serious look.

"Do you think Princess Sugar Plum will be safe before we can get to her?" Clara asked with concern.

Prince Dustin took a long time to answer as if he were thinking about how to respond to Clara, without getting her more frightened. "Egon is evil and is out for vengeance. He is not interested in harming Sugar Plum."

Clara gulped as she read between the lines of what Prince Dustin was saying. "Then she should be safe until we arrive," Clara said. Her eyes moved from left to right.

"Yes, I believe so," Prince Dustin responded.

"But Clara, about your Unc—" Before Prince Dustin could finish his sentence, a small bear-like animal jumped out from behind the trees.

The animal was no larger than a small stuffed toy. Its fur was smooth, golden brown, the color of toast. It had big doll-like brown eyes and a black nose. It looked like a baby bear, Clara thought. It jumped up and down and turned all around in front of them as if it wanted to play.

"Look! Isn't it adorable?" Clara said as she pointed at the little animal. Clara bent down to cuddle the small bear-like creature behind its little ears. Clara thought its ear felt like a cotton ball.

Prince Dustin pulled Clara back. "Clara, we are deeper in the Black Forest. Things aren't always as they appear."

Clara quickly jumped backward. She politely apologized after colliding into Bronson. Bronson grunted softly.

The General barked quick, short barks, communicating something to Prince Dustin. Of course, Clara did not understand. She did notice that the General didn't look tense at all. His eyes were not scanning the area, and his tail was relaxed.

"The General said that it won't hurt you, Clara." Prince Dustin smiled. "It's a Knuddelig. The General said they like to cuddle and play." Prince Dustin bent down and rubbed the little animal behind its ears. The animal started making coo-like sounds.

COO   COO   COO

"It sounds like a baby." Clara giggled. "It's so cute!"

Just then, rustling sounds were heard from behind trees. "Is it a baby?" Clara said cautiously, looking around for the animal's mother.

The General barked, quick short barks.

"The General said that it is fully grown." Prince Dustin relayed as he continued to rub the little animal behind its ears.

Clara tickled the Knuddelig's belly. It started cooing as if it were laughing.

A-COO   A-COO   A-COO

"I wish I could take him home with me." Clara's eyes sparkled.

The rustling noise continued as more Knuddeligs came out from behind the trees. They jumped up and down on Clara. Clara laughed and laughed. She played with the Knuddeligs for several minutes, before the little animals scampered off.

As Clara watched the little animals depart, she noticed that the General, Bronson and Prince Dustin seemed to be having a serious conversation. *Something is wrong,* Clara thought.

The General communicated something to Prince Dustin. Clara didn't know what the General conveyed, but she assumed it was not good, by the look on Prince Dustin's face. Prince Dustin nodded from time to time and looked into the trees behind them.

Is something wicked in the trees? Is that why my little friends left? Clara wondered. *Did they sense danger?*

Clara hadn't noticed, but the sun was no longer peeking through the canopy of branches. Although it was still morning, the forest had become dark–very, very dark.

Clara thought she saw a thick fog in the distance, between the trees.

"Clara!"

Clara jumped. She noticed that Prince Dustin was gripping the handle of his sword.

"We must move quickly, Clara."

"I'm right behind you," Clara replied.

Although Prince Dustin had looked back at Clara, Clara noticed that his eyes were looking behind her, into the trees. Clara turned her head around to see what had alerted Prince Dustin. A gray fog was tunneling through the trees. It seemed to be following them. Clara noticed that the General's ears were sticking straight up. They looked like they were vibrating, Clara thought.

Prince Dustin and Bronson moved quickly between the trees. Clara ran behind them. The General followed behind Clara.

"Watch out for that branch," Prince Dustin said, looking back at Clara. A large limb had broken off a tree and was on the ground. Clara nodded as she avoided tripping over the fallen branch. She did not stop. She ran as fast as she could.

Clara heard animals all around. The animals didn't sound friendly. The animals were not purring or cooing. They were not chirping, hooting, or even tweeting. The animals were screeching, wailing and hissing. Clara ran even faster, yet.

Then Clara heard a deep hum. The sound was coming from behind them. The humming was coming from the fog.

HUM

-8-

Schmetterling Butterflies

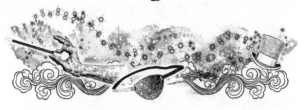

The fog was after them. They continued to run through the forest trying to escape. Something was in the fog, and it was headed straight for them.

They kept running, without slowing down.

After a short while, Prince Dustin glanced back at Clara. "Clara, are we running too fast?" Prince Dustin said as he shot Clara a glance over his shoulder.

Clara was moving slower. "I-I'll try to keep up." Clara panted.

Prince Dustin looked at Bronson, "We have to give Clara a moment to catch her breath." Bronson grunted and slowed his pace.

"What is in the fog? Is it coming after us?" Clara asked, leaning against a tree. She was breathing heavy. Her hair was dripping wet, and sweat poured down from her forehead.

"Whatever it is, it is moving slower now," Prince Dustin said, looking into the trees. "It should have caught up to us."

Clara nodded. Her chest was heaving up and down. "Do you think it wants to hurt us?" Clara figured she already knew the answer, but asked, anyway. The General barked. Bronson grunted.

"The General said that he hasn't seen anything like it before. He thinks it could be an evil force."

Clara blew out of the side of her mouth and tried to appear brave. She said with concern, "I-I think it frightened those little bears." Prince Dustin nodded. Clara noticed that the General's ears stood straight and his tail was fully extended.

"Clara are you able to continue? We want to put distance between us and the fog."

Clara noticed that Prince Dustin was not looking at her, but into the trees. Clara followed Prince Dustin's eyes. Her eyes went wide, and she sprung forward. "It's getting closer."

"Let's go," Prince Dustin said. The others quickly followed behind Prince Dustin.

The gray fog hovered above the ground and barreled between the trees. It seemed to be getting thicker and faster. It seemed to be sucking up the earth as it traveled. Clara ran as fast as she could to keep up with Prince Dustin. Occasionally she heard Prince Dustin call out her name. His voice was muffled by all the other sounds.

Sounds were coming from all directions. The animals in the trees were screeching, wailing and hissing. *Maybe they are afraid of what's in the fog,* Clara thought. Clara couldn't see any of the animals making the sounds. They were hidden behind the branches. An unnerving thought crossed her mind. *Maybe they aren't animals at all.*

The humming sound got louder. Clara looked back. *Whatever is in the fog must be getting closer!* The humming did not start and stop, like something catching its breath. It was a monotone flat, dull, continuous hum. *It is after us!*

Clara cupped her ears. She didn't want to hear the hum.

Bronson grunted. It sounded like a roar. Clara jumped. It scared her as much as the sounds coming from the trees. Clara wanted to look behind them to see what made Bronson roar. *What is out there? What is in the fog!* Clara kept running, without looking back.

Clara didn't hear any sounds coming from The General. *Is the General still behind us? Did it get the General?* Clara slowed her pace and looked back. Her hand trembled as she tucked her hair out of her face.

Clara glared at the General. His fangs glistened with drool. *Whatever is in the fog, it did not get the General,* Clara thought, relieved. She then looked behind the General. The fog was thundering toward them. Clara jerked her head around and ran faster.

Clara did not look right or left. She just ran. The hum drowned out the sounds of the animals. Clara pressed her hands hard to her ears, but she still heard the hum. Prince Dustin led them around trees over rocks, and over a small creek. Clara glanced back from time to time. The gray fog was still behind them as they charged through the forest.

Without any notice, Prince Dustin slowed his pace. The others slowed down, too.

"Look there." Prince Dustin stopped. He pointed at the sky ahead.

Bronson stared ahead. His nose twitched, and his mouth was wide open. His two big front teeth hung over his lower lip.

The General stopped and barked several times. Clara glanced at the General and Bronson with a confused look. *I wish I could talk to the animals.* Clara sighed.

Clara blinked and tilted her head. I don't hear the hum anymore. She bit her lip and glanced over her shoulder. *The fog is gone!* Clara looked over at Prince Dustin wondering if he'd noticed that the fog was no longer behind them. Prince Dustin was still looking at the sky ahead.

Clara rubbed the side of her face then took a quick look over her shoulder, again. She did not see the fog. *Is it gone?* She wondered. Clara looked over at the General. She noticed that he was no longer baring his teeth. The General barked twice as if responding to Clara's thoughts.

"Look at the purple mist in the air," Prince Dustin said, pointing.

Clara looked ahead. A purple mist glowed across the horizon. The mist seemed to be lively and playful. Flecks of gold shimmered in the purple haze. Clara gazed dreamily at the purple cloud. It reminded her of flower crocuses in a field.

"It looks like a purple cloud." Clara's eyes glimmered. "Something gold is twirling in it," Clara said, twirling her finger in circles. "And what's that music?" Soft music was coming from the purple cloud.

The General barked.

"The General said that we are in the Land of the Butterflies," Prince Dustin said. "They are called Schmetterling butterflies."

"Butterflies?" Clara glowed with excitement.

The General barked again.

Clara frowned. She wished she could understand the General. She noticed that Prince Dustin was smiling as he listened to the General.

"Yes, butterflies. Because there are so many of them, they look like a purple cloud," Prince Dustin said. "The General said that their wings have gold specks so when they fly it looks like something is twirling."

Clara's eyes lit up. She grinned from ear to ear. "It looks like gold dust floating in a purple cloud."

Prince Dustin nodded. "I guess it does look like that, Clara."

"Can we go look at them close up?" Clara skipped toward the cloud of butterflies, without waiting for a reply.

"Sure." Prince Dustin followed behind Clara. Bronson and the General joined Prince Dustin.

The butterflies floated above. The sound of a harp could be heard coming from the cloud of butterflies. Clara was in a daze as she skipped toward the cloud of butterflies. Thousands of purple butterflies floated in the air. The closer Clara got to the butterflies, the better she heard the soft music.

The cloud of purple butterflies moved toward Clara, as if to greet her. Clara's eyes glistened. She marveled at the sight of the delicate purple and gold butterflies.

Clara thought about her ballet class. Miss Patti would invite local musicians to accompany the class. One time, a musician played the harp. Clara looked at the butterflies. *The music sounds like a harp.* Clara moved her fingers like she was strumming a harp.

Prince Dustin, Bronson, and the General watched Clara and the butterflies from a short distance away. The cloud of butterflies floated around Clara.

Clara looked up and stretched out her arms. She turned around and around and around to the sound of the music. She kept turning around, as if she were flying in the middle of the cloud of butterflies. After several turns around, a single butterfly landed on the tip of Clara's nose. Clara tried not to move. She looked at the butterfly with crossed-eyes.

"Hello, little butterfly," Clara whispered. She thought she heard the sound of the music get louder. Clara smiled at the little butterfly.

The butterfly fluttered its wings but did not fly away.

"Can you understand me, little butterfly?" Clara said softly. She stood as still as possible looking at the butterfly on her nose. She didn't want it to fly away. Clara thought she heard the music get even louder, in a soft kind of way.

"la la la la la la la la la la la la la"

Prince Dustin, Bronson, and the General watched as Clara spoke to the little butterfly on her nose. The General barked softly, communicating something to Prince Dustin and Bronson.

"You are the most beautiful butterfly I've ever seen," Clara said to the little butterfly. The little butterfly moved its antennas, as if it understood Clara.

"I wish I could speak to animals. I would speak to birds, and puppies, kittens and guppies, and of course, beautiful butterflies." Clara batted her eyes at the little butterfly. The little butterfly fluttered its wings.

Then suddenly—the cloud of purple butterflies spun and twirled. The butterflies spun so fast around Clara, Clara got dizzy. The vibration from their wings played music that got louder and louder the faster they spun. The music sounded like a lullaby. *They are dancing!* Clara was amazed.

The butterflies formed a cocoon around Clara.

Prince Dustin, Bronson, and the General sat on the grass gazing at the butterflies. They were motionless as if hypnotized by the swirling.

Clara stood in the middle of the butterflies. They danced around Clara like a waltz—*The Waltz of the Butterflies.* THEN—

THUMP

Clara's eyes rolled back in her head, and she fell to the ground.

-9-

Niedertrachtig Castle

The halls of Niedertrachtig Castle were dreadful and smelled of decaying animals. The castle had been vacant for almost a century, after a mysterious incident surrounding the disappearance of the Duke and Duchess. Evil was thought to live within the walls of the castle.

Everything inside the castle was in the exact place as it was on that tragic day when the Duke and Duchess disappeared. Travelers that passed through the area often told stories of seeing dark shadows and flickering lights through the arched windows in the tower. People said that the wind whipped around the castle making a hissing sound—as if it were possessed by a dark power wanting to get out.

❖ ❖ ❖

"Dusty has three days to bring Clara." Egon's nostrils flared as he stomped down the hall, speaking to Drosselmeyer. Egon's face was distorted in the dim light. His tail slashed through the air. His short red, velvet cape and jeweled crown seemed out of place on his huge body.

"Oh yes, their precious little Clara," Drosselmeyer responded. Walking down the hall of Niedertrachtig Castle, he was partly-hidden behind Egon. Drosselmeyer pulled at his black cape, hastening his step.

The two sinister-looking figures walked comfortably through the corridors. It was as though the evil that was inside the castle welcomed them.

Egon cursed. "My brother would still be alive had it not been for that, that little girl—" Egon paused. He stopped at a hall mirror and looked at his reflection. He wiped the dust off the mirror for a better view. Egon adjusted his crown and tilted his right shoulder forward. He smiled, obviously pleased with his reflection.

Egon was massive. Standing on his hind legs, he stood taller than most men. Although his body was muscular, his belly was large and round. His razor-sharp whiskers stuck straight out from each side of his muzzle.

"Prince Dustin and Clara should get here by the day after." Drosselmeyer looked at his reflection in the mirror. His pale blue eyes looked white.

"Prince Dustin?" Egon said with disgust, interrupting Drosselmeyer. "You mean, Dusty," Egon added, as if he disapproved of Prince Dustin being called a prince.

Drosselmeyer bowed his head. "Yes, I meant, Dusty."

"And they thought their little Prince was going to be King." Egon spat on the floor.

Drosselmeyer raised his right brow and stepped over the spit.

Egon continued, "And you, Dross ... what do you stand to gain?"

Drosselmeyer did not immediately answer. He closed his eyes for a moment. Because his eyes were as white as his skin, it didn't look like he had closed his eyes at all. "You are not the only one who seeks revenge," Drosselmeyer finally responded.

Egon nodded without inquiring further. The muscles in his powerful hind legs bulged as he stepped.

They continued down the hall in silence. Each of them appeared to be grinning, as if each were relishing thoughts of their own sweet revenge.

The only sound that could be heard was the sound of Egon's heavy footsteps echoing off the castle's walls.

❖ ❖ ❖

Down, down deep in the dungeon of Niedertrachtig Castle was a small chamber with a heavy wooden door. The door had a small window with closely held wooden bars. To the right of the door, a crystal sconce hung on the wall. A sliver of light from the crystal filtered through the bars into the room.

Crouched in a far corner of the small room, on the dirt floor, Princess Sugar Plum looked for a way out. She was still dressed in the white gown that she had chosen for Prince Dustin's coronation.

She kept recounting the events that happened the day before, over and over in her mind: She was about to put on her tiara when she heard people shuffling into her bedroom. She had thought it was someone coming to tell her that it was time for her to perform for the ceremony.

By the time she saw Egon out of the corner of her eye, it was too late. He quickly wrapped a blanket around her and flung her over his shoulder. She did not have time to fly away. As a tree fairy, she was always able to fly away to avoid danger. *Why didn't I turn around sooner?*

Someone was with Egon, but Princess Sugar Plum could not see who it was because of the blanket wrapped around her. She heard the other person tell Egon to put something inside the blanket, leaves from a plant. Sugar Plum remembered that the leaves smelled pungent.

Princess Sugar Plum recounted getting sleepy then. She could still hear voices, but the words were not clear. The last thing Sugar Plum remembered hearing was that they were taking her to a castle deeper in the Black Forest. She heard them say Prince Dustin would bring Clara there in three days.

I have to come up with a plan. We can't let Egon get Clara, Princess Sugar Plum thought.

-10-

Magic in the Air

Prince Dustin jumped as Clara fell to the ground. "Clara!" Prince Dustin snapped out of his trance and darted toward Clara. After Clara fell to the ground, the music continued at a slower beat as the butterflies flew away. A single butterfly remained, fluttering. It flew away when Prince Dustin reached Clara.

"Clara! Clara!" Prince Dustin panicked. Clara was motionless on the ground. Her face was pale, and her lips had turned a tinge purple. Bronson and the General were now by Prince Dustin's side. Bronson grunted not knowing what to do. The General started barking, communicating something. Prince

Dustin listened without his eyes leaving Clara. He saw that Clara was breathing.

"She's breathing," Prince Dustin said with relief.

The General barked twice. Bronson cradled Clara's head on his soft brown fur like a pillow. Although Clara's eyes were closed, she was breathing normally. She looked like she was asleep.

"Color is coming back to her face," Prince Dustin said. He watched as Clara began to open her eyes.

"What happened?" Clara said surprised. Everyone stared at Clara with concern. Her eyes were glossed over as she raised her head. She looked up at Bronson and smiled. She thought he felt like a big fluffy pillow. Before Prince Dustin could answer, Clara continued, "Did I have another dream?"

Prince Dustin opened his mouth to speak but paused. Prince Dustin was always so protective of Clara and probably didn't want to scare her by telling her what happened.

Clara sat up and looked around. "Where did the butterflies go?"

"They flew away, Clara," the General said. "They flew across the meadow and beyond those trees. I can't hear their music anymore," the General continued as he pointed toward the trees in the distance, across the field.

Clara tilted her head toward the field. She did not hear any music. "I can't hear them either," she said. "Their music reminded me of my dance class."

"Did you like their music, Clara?" the General said, rubbing his right ear with his front paw. He continued, "When there's a celebration at the Ice Palace, Queen Nordika has musicians play soft music. It sounds like the music the butterflies make."

"The Ice Palace reminds me of my dollhouse." Clara then laughed, "I had expected it to be made out of ice. The palace is lovely, just like Queen Nordika," Clara said, smiling at the General. "I would imagine the celebrations are quite festive."

"Yes, they are, Clara," the General replied. Clara smiled.

The General continued, "Schmetterling butterflies are special butterflies, even for the Black Forest," the General said, exchanging glances with Prince Dustin and Bronson. "They have magical powers, Clara,"

"Magical butterflies?" Clara said, sounding astonished. Clara leaned forward toward the General and gazed at him with rapt attention.

"Yes, Clara," the General said.

"What kind of magical powers?" Clara's eyes sparkled, and she was speaking fast. Excitement could be heard in her voice. "I hope they come back soon." Clara craned her neck and peered into the trees looking for the butterflies.

"They are gone," the General said. "I don't think they are coming back."

"Why not?" Clara said, disappointed.

The General spoke softly, "Because they already used their magic here, Clara."

Clara looked around and didn't see any signs of the gray fog. "Do you think they used their magic on the fog?" Clara said, pointing at the trees behind them. "I was wondering what happened to that fog. It was pretty scary."

A smile froze on Prince Dustin's face. Bronson remained silent. They both stared at the General waiting for his reply.

"Yes, that too," the General said, with his mouth open and his lips turned up.

Clara's eyes and mouth shot wide open. She held both her cheeks with the palms of her hands and stared at the General. "G-general," Clara said, stuttering. "I can understand you!"

"Yes, Clara. It would appear so," the General said, nodding his head.

"They must have used their magic on you, Clara," Bronson said.

"I can understand you too, Bronson!" Clara said, astonished.

Prince Dustin smiled at Clara and confirmed, "They used their magical powers on you, Clara."

"I-I can now talk to animals!" Clara jumped to her feet with joy. She turned around in a pirouette. "Say something, Bronson."

"What would you like me to say, Clara?"

"Yes!" Clara clenched her hands and looked up at the blue sky. "I can understand, you, Bronson. You said, 'What would you like me to say, Clara?' Right?" Clara glowed.

Bronson replied, "That is what I said, Clara."

"But how can this be?" Clara said after calming down.

"Schmetterlings have the power to grant wishes," the General said. "That butterfly that landed on your nose, Clara—"

"Yes," Clara twisted her nose, as if wondering what the General was about to say.

"I heard you tell the butterfly that you wished you could talk to animals like Prince Dustin," the General added.

"Yes, I did say that to that little butterfly." Clara smiled with glee, touching her nose.

"They granted your wish, Clara," Prince Dustin interjected. "You can now speak to animals."

Clara was speechless.

-11-

Herr Drosselmeyer

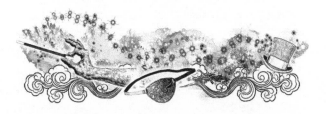

They had gone even deeper into the Black Forest since they left the Land of the Butterflies. The sun was no longer shining—at least not here. Although it was not yet evening, the skies were dark and gray. The clouds had all departed or had been eaten by the sky.

The trees look alive! Clara grimaced as they moved between spindly trees that loomed up from the ground in the forest. These trees were spaced far apart, not dense like the pine trees in other parts of the Black Forest. *I have never seen trees like these before.* Clara gasped.

The General was leading them now. He slowed their pace. Clara walked slower than the others. The ground had barely any grass, and what was there was wheat-brown dead. The spindly trees were shorter, unlike the other trees in the forest. They did not reach the sky. Their slender trunks and limbs were bare, with very little bark. Clara thought their branches were the creepiest part of all.

Clara tried not to look but found herself staring at the limbs of the spindly trees. Clara noticed that they waved in the air, however—there was no wind. The branches of the trees seemed to be grasping for something. Clara tried to stay a good distance away but kept feeling herself being drawn toward the trees.

"Come here."

Alarmed, Clara stumbled and took a step backward. She thought she heard a voice coming from one of the trees. Prince Dustin glanced at Clara with a concerned look. Clara smiled at Prince Dustin as if nothing was wrong.

Clara stared at the tree. Its twisted limbs were gnarly-looking and ash-gray. The tree had barely a leaf. The limbs and branches of the tree bent at the middle, almost like elbows of an arm. Clara shrugged as she stared at the tree. She thought she heard the soft child-like voice continue. She shook her head and said silently, *Trees don't talk.*

"Come play with me." The soft voice coming from the tree continued as it waved for Clara to come closer.

Clara stood in shock and repeated silently, *Trees don't talk.*

"Come here. I promise I won't hurt you, little girl. I just want to play. Come closer so we can play."

Clara heard the tree speak again. With glazed eyes, Clara walked toward the tree. Her slippers sunk into the ground with each step. The limbs of the tree waved its branches like arms, summoning Clara closer and closer. Clara moved closer to the tree without blinking her eyes.

"That's right little girl, come closer. Let's play."

Clara seemed to be in a trance. The closer she moved toward the tree, the less child-like the tree sounded. Clara continued walking slowly toward the tree. With each step, her foot sunk deeper and deeper into the ground.

"That's right, just a little closer, little girl. Come on, just a couple of more steps," the tree continued. It's branches almost reached Clara as it waved. Clara stepped closer and closer to the tree.

"Clara!" Prince Dustin must have noticed Clara acting oddly and quickly ran over to her.

Hearing Prince Dustin, Clara shook her head as though she were snapping out of a trance. She stared with bug eyes at Prince Dustin. "Yes," Clara replied.

"Clara, we have to be careful deeper in the Black Forest," Prince Dustin said with alarm. He shot a glance at the tree that Clara was wandering toward, and then directed Clara away from the tree. Bronson and the General joined Prince Dustin. They looked at Clara. Worry could be seen in their eyes.

"We better rest," Prince Dustin said. "Over there, under that spruce tree." Prince Dustin spotted one of the few evergreen trees in this part of the forest. "We have traveled quite a distance and have not had a break since we left the Land of the Butterflies."

Bronson added, "You are probably exhausted, Clara."

"I-I just wanted to take a closer look at that tree," Clara stuttered as she sat down. "The trees are different here than the ones in the rest of the Black Forest."

Clara looked across the clearing and glared back at the spindly tree. She listened. She no longer heard voices coming from the tree. She looked at everyone, "Thank you, I am fine." *Trees don't talk,* Clara said silently.

Bronson began telling tales about life on the river. Prince Dustin and the General laughed at the stories Bronson told about the beavers.

Clara glanced at the spindly tree again. She hoped that none of the others noticed. The tree was waving its limbs, as if summoning Clara to come back. Clara jerked and positioned herself with her back toward the spindly tree. Clara then laughed at whatever Bronson said, although she had not heard him at all.

They sat under the spruce tree longer than they had planned. After a while, Clara noticed that the forest was quiet. She did not hear the sound of any of the animals that she had heard earlier. Clara sighed. *Now that I can talk to animals, there aren't any animals to talk to.*

Clara no longer considered the General or Bronson as a shepherd or beaver. They were *just like her*, she thought. She never once thought that maybe she was becoming *just like them*. She never thought that maybe she was becoming part of the Black Forest.

"I have something that I have been meaning to convey to you, Clara," Prince Dustin said in a serious tone.

"Is it Princess Sugar Plum?" Clara said, half-rising. Clara continued, "I am rested now. I can continue. We have to get to her."

Prince Dustin responded, "I am presuming that Princess Sugar Plum is fine for the moment." He paused before continuing, "It is something else." Prince Dustin pulled at the hem of his jacket and lowered his head.

Clara sensed the seriousness of Prince Dustin's tone. "Is it Queen Nordika? Did Egon hurt Queen Nordika?"

"Queen Nordika is fine," Prince Dustin said with a convincing tone. "It's not her."

Clara rubbed the palms of her hands together. "I don't understand. If it is not about Princess Sugar Plum or Queen Nordika, Bronson and the General are here with us," Clara paused before continuing, "then who?"

"It is Herr Drosselmeyer," Prince Dustin said. "Your Uncle Drosselmeyer."

"My Uncle Drosselmeyer?" Clara said with a surprised tone.

Bronson looked at Clara with sympathetic eyes. "I am sorry, Clara."

"We were all surprised, especially Queen Nordika," the General added.

"Did Egon hurt my Uncle Drosselmeyer?" Clara shrieked. Prince Dustin exchanged glances with Bronson and the General. He looked sideways, as if trying to find the right words. Clara looked hysterical. "Did Egon hurt my Uncle Drosselmeyer?" she repeated.

Prince Dustin looked at Clara. "I wanted to tell you earlier, Clara."

Clara asked, "Is my Uncle Drosselmeyer okay?"

Prince Dustin shook his head and placed his hand on Clara's shoulder.

Clara glanced at Prince Dustin then at Bronson. Bronson hung his head.

Prince Dustin continued, "We don't know what happened. We were all taken by surprise." Clara could sense that Prince

Dustin was having a hard time telling her what happened to her Uncle Drosselmeyer. She knew it had to be something terrible. She no longer wanted to hear the news.

"Egon did not hurt your Uncle Drosselmeyer," Prince Dustin said. Clara looked even more confused. "Did you hear me, Clara?" Prince Dustin asked softly.

Clara nodded.

Prince Dustin continued, "Your Uncle Drosselmeyer kidnapped Princess Sugar Plum." Prince Dustin looked at Clara without blinking. "Herr Drosselmeyer and Egon kidnapped Sugar Plum," Prince Dustin said as he pulled at the hem of his jacket.

Clara's face dropped. She did not want to believe what she heard. "Egon! Egon kidnapped Princess Sugar Plum, right?" Clara looked at Prince Dustin with desperation.

"I am sorry, Clara," Prince Dustin said. "Herr Drosselmeyer deceived us all. He and Egon kidnapped Sugar Plum."

"But, why? Why would my Uncle Drosselmeyer kidnap Princess Sugar Plum?"

"We do not, as yet, know the full story," Prince Dustin replied. "Queen Nordika said that Herr Drosselmeyer is very old. Nobody knows the number of years." Clara leaned forward, listening.

Prince Dustin continued, "She said that a long, long time ago, many things happened deeper in the Black Forest. The forces of good and evil clashed, much of which remains a secret."

Clara felt her head spinning. "So, my Uncle Drosselmeyer was pretending all this time."

"Yes, Clara. He was pretending."

Clara shook her head in shock. Although her eyes turned red, she did not cry. She held back her tears.

Prince Dustin continued, "With Egon and Herr Drosselmeyer joining forces, their evil could have very dire consequences for all of the Black Forest. We must stop them." Prince Dustin stood after completing his sentence.

Clara leaped to her feet. "I'm ready."

-12-

Mistake by
Mother Nature

They walked briskly through the forest. None seemed to hear any of the animal sounds. Prince Dustin had been quiet for this leg of the trip. He finally broke the silence and said, "I have put everyone in danger." He continued, "I should have suspected that Herr Drosselmeyer was evil. I did not notice any signs that he was being deceptive. How did I not know? I should have known."

Clara saw beads of sweat on Prince Dustin's forehead. She opened her mouth to speak. Clara wanted to tell Prince Dustin that it was not his fault. Before she could say a word, Prince Dustin continued with sad eyes.

"Clara, Princess Sugar Plum, and every person and animal living in the Black Forest, I put everyone in danger."

Clara again opened her mouth to speak, but before she could say a word, Prince Dustin turned toward everyone.

Prince Dustin faced everyone with his chin up and head high. "First, we will save Sugar Plum. Then, we will save the Black Forest!" His eyes did not blink, and his mouth did not quiver. Bronson and the General bowed their heads in allegiance.

Prince Dustin looked like a warrior going into battle, fighting an enemy that he had beaten before. Prince Dustin charged forward. The others followed.

They continued through the forest. After walking for a long time, they rested. Prince Dustin communicated to the others his plan for rescuing Princess Sugar Plum and saving the Black Forest. Occasionally Bronson and the General added comments. Although Clara did not say a word, her eyes were focused and resolute. The afternoon sun began to fade, and dusk was on the horizon.

Just as the sky turned gray, the wind picked up. It wasn't gradual, but quite sudden, as if a storm was looming. Clara looked up but didn't see or hear any signs of thunder or lightning. *That's odd*, Clara thought.

Bronson's actions caught Clara's attention. She stared at him with alarm. Bronson's fur was no longer lying flat, and his small ears were quivering. His front teeth gleamed and protruded past his lips. Clara also noticed that he was jerking his head and sniffing.

Clara remembered seeing Bronson like this last Christmas Eve when she had gotten separated from Prince Dustin. Bronson had taken her inside a cave. She remembered hearing an eerie clapping sound in the cave.

CLAP CLAP CLAP CLAP CLAP

It was the sound the cave creatures made when they flapped their wings. The translucent creatures had jointed wings that made a clapping sound when they flew. Clara's face froze as she remembered. A crunching sound in the trees snapped Clara back to the present. *Something's in the trees!*

Prince Dustin stood slowly and withdrew his sword.

Clara shot to her feet. She heard the General say, "... we will not be able to outrun them!" She glanced at Prince Dustin with desperate eyes.

Prince Dustin lifted his heels from the ground. However, he was too weak to fly. He turned toward Clara, "My strength has not been fully restored, I am unable to fly. Since I am not a Tree Fairy, I can only fly with my full strength." Clara nodded. She remembered that from before.

Prince Dustin looked around in a sweeping fashion as if he were contemplating their options. The wind blew stronger. It was coming from the trees. Prince Dustin removed his sword from its sheath. "We will take that path," he added, pointing his sword to a path ahead as he led them. Clara followed close behind. Bronson and the General followed behind Clara. The General's ears perked as he listened to the sounds coming from the trees.

The path they took quickly ended, and they found themselves weaving around spruce and fir trees. The terrain was not level, and Clara kept tripping over fallen branches and dips in the ground. Clara wished that Prince Dustin had the strength to fly so that they could fly away from whatever was creating that fierce wind behind them. Prince Dustin glanced back at Clara and slowed his pace. Something moved quickly pass them.

SWOOSH

Clara stopped in her tracks. Bronson almost collided with her. Prince Dustin turned around. He looked at Clara with puzzled eyes. Clara's mouth was wide open, and her finger shook as she pointed to something in front of Prince Dustin.

Prince Dustin turned his head back around. A horrible greenish-brown creature, the size of a raccoon, stared back at Prince Dustin. It raised its tail and rattled it like a snake. Prince Dustin pointed his sword at the greenish-brown creature.

"What is that?" Prince Dustin gawked, turning his head slightly toward the General. His eyes showed relief as if he were glad the animal was no bigger. The animal stood its ground. Its rat-shaped head resembled that of a possum, and its slimy skin was a murky green and brown, like a scorpion.

Clara thought the animal looked like a mistake by Mother Nature. *It looks worse than the cave creatures,* Clara thought. The creature had six legs and a pair of grasping claws. Its rattling tail was curved and segmented. It snapped its front claws at Clara, as though it could read her thoughts. Clara jumped.

The hideous animal seemed to mock Prince Dustin. It appeared to glare at Prince Dustin with a smirk on its face. When Prince Dustin moved his head to the right, the creature moved its cone-shaped head to the right. When Prince Dustin moved his head left, the creature did the same.

"Clara, move back slowly," Prince Dustin said with caution. Before Clara could move, the creature rattled its tail, raised its claws and snapped viciously. Clara did not move. "Move back, Clara."

The General jumped in front of Clara. Clara moved back. Prince Dustin raised his sword above his head with both hands. He did not take his eyes off the animal. Bronson moved toward Prince Dustin. The creature snapped its claws at Bronson as if warning Bronson to stay back.

Bronson kept his eyes on the creature. The fur on Bronson's neck stood up as he moved in slow steps toward Prince Dustin. He and Prince Dustin nodded at each other as if they were communicating something without speaking a word. The creature hissed then lunged at Prince Dustin and Bronson.

Clara shrieked. She feverishly looked on the ground for a rock to throw at the creature. With slow, deliberate steps, Bronson inched closer and closer toward the creature with his rudder-like tail held high off the ground. He looked over at Prince Dustin. Prince Dustin nodded.

Bronson then charged forward, toward the creature. The creature appeared surprised. For a brief moment, it stopped rattling its tail and snapping its claws. It raised its head and made a shrill-hissing sound.

Before the animal could move, Bronson leaped in the air and slammed his rudder-like tail on the animal. Prince Dustin held his sword high. The General barked a low, deep gruff.

Bronson then peered over his shoulder and lifted his tail with caution. The creature was flat on its back from being slammed. The creature's legs wriggled and flailed above its body. One of the creature's claws dangled from its side and moved back and forth like a pendulum.

Prince Dustin did not delay. He pulled his sword back, then with a powerful strike, lunged forward, and stabbed the creature. Green slime oozed out of the creature's belly. Prince Dustin yanked his sword out of the creature's body, wiping its blade on the grass. The creature made a gurgling sound as green slime dribbled out of its mouth.

Clara turned and vomited from the smell. She hoped nobody noticed as she wiped her mouth. Clara looked back at the creature. It was no longer moving. The claw that was dangling fell off its body and rolled toward Bronson. Bronson kicked the claw hard, and it vaulted into the trees.

Clara's eyes followed the dismembered claw until it was lost in the branches of the trees. Prince Dustin scanned the area, possibly looking for other creatures. He then thrust his sword back into its sheath. "It does smell awful, Clara. I could barely keep my stomach from churning," Prince Dustin said with a sympathetic voice.

"Uhm, yes," Clara responded in a nasal tone, holding her nose.

Prince Dustin said, "Let's move on. I can't take this smell much longer." Bronson grunted, and the General barked several times.

Prince Dustin and Clara were back in front as they walked through the forest at a fast pace. Bronson, possibly trying to lighten the mood to get Clara's mind off the creature, recalled when the mouse soldiers were captured on the frozen moat around Queen Nordika's Ice Palace.

"Their legs were tangled, and they kept slipping and sliding over their tails on the ice." Clara laughed, recalling the event.

Prince Dustin added, "Queen Nordika's army took them by surprise."

"I couldn't even see her army. You blended in with the snow," Clara said looking at the General.

The General replied, "Camouflage is one of our best weapons, Clara. We try to avoid battles whenever possible, so we use the element of surprise to capture foes and challengers."

"The shepherds are quite fierce. Most animals in the Black Forest run just from their bark," Prince Dustin added. The General stood with pride at Prince Dustin's remark.

Clara smiled. "—and those little shepherd puppies. They were so cute."

The General's eyes beamed. "Thank you, Clara. Those puppies are my offspring."

"Queen Nordika's future army," Prince Dustin added.

"I don't know why the puppies stayed away from Bronson." Clara glanced at Bronson. "They don't know you as I do, I guess. When you rescued me—well, after I figured out you weren't going to eat me—I thought you were quite kind," Clara said, tripping over her words.

The General added mockingly, "Yes ... Bronson is so sweet and cuddly."

Bronson grunted at being called, 'sweet and cuddly.' Everyone laughed, but Bronson.

Clara was surprised that the General made a funny remark. *The General always seems quite focused*, she thought quietly.

They continued to talk and laugh as they journeyed through the forest. Clara noticed that after a short time, the General positioned himself behind the group and remained quiet. His ears stood straight up, and his eyes moved from side to side.

Clara reasoned that if anything approached them, the General would know far in advance. Clara looked back and smiled at the General.

Clara walked as if she didn't have a care in the world. She forgot about Egon. She forgot about her Uncle Drosselmeyer. She forgot about the cave creatures and human-sized mice. Clara hummed a tune all the girls sang back in her hometown. Clara forgot that she was deeper in the Black Forest.

"la la la la la"

"Don't move!" Prince Dustin extended his arm, shielding Clara. Clara gasped.

-13-

Little Fairy Princess

Egon and Drosselmeyer were in the dungeon of Niedertrachtig Castle. Egon looked through the bars of the small window of one of the chambers. He cocked his head to the side and rubbed his neck. His black eyes glistened like patent leather. "She looks like she is dressed for a ball," Egon said to Drosselmeyer with a sinister laugh.

Princess Sugar Plum did not look up. She refused to let Egon see the tears that had welled up in her eyes. Hearing Egon made her skin crawl. She squirmed on the cellar's floor.

"Tsk tsk—her white dress has gotten dirty," Egon said, feigning concern.

Drosselmeyer whipped his cape to the side and glanced over Egon's shoulder. He peered through the bars at Princess Sugar Plum. His eyes showed no hint of emotion. Sensing Drosselmeyer, Princess Sugar Plum glared at the barred window on the chamber's door.

"Poor little fairy princess," Egon said, cackling.

Princess Sugar Plum lowered her head. She still could not believe that Herr Drosselmeyer joined forces with Egon.

"I believe the little fairy princess is crying, Dross. It gets me right here." Egon raised his head and placed his clawed paws over his heart. His pointed claws were stained black. His crown slid down to his forehead. Egon used the tip of one of his nails to move it back in place.

Drosselmeyer laughed.

Egon continued, "Now, now—you are not being a polite guest. Don't they teach you manners in princess school?"

Drosselmeyer clasped his hands behind his back. Princess Sugar Plum clenched her fists into a ball, without looking up.

"I find it quite rude that you have not greeted me with a proper curtsy. Aren't princesses taught to curtsy before their King?"

"You are not my King!" Princess Sugar Plum retorted.

Egon adjusted his cape and glanced over at Drosselmeyer with a smug look, "I think I may have hurt her feelings."

"When my brother gets here—" Princess Sugar Plum started.

Egon forced his full face to the bars of the window, interrupting Princess Sugar Plum. "I can't wait. That's when the party starts." He then shot an evil wink at Princess Sugar Plum.

Drosselmeyer nodded without regard. Princess Sugar Plum glared with raised eyebrows at the barred window, as if wondering what Egon meant by his remark.

"It would appear that I have her attention now," Egon sneered.

"I think so," Drosselmeyer replied.

Herr Drosselmeyer, what happened to you? Princess Sugar Plum flinched.

Egon nodded at Drosselmeyer. "Uh, getting back to the party. Clara will be our honored guest, for dinner."

We can't let him hurt Clara. Sugar Plum sighed.

"The Black Forest will be such a better place without that little girl around," Egon said. "She should have minded her own business."

"Prince Dustin is not going to let you hurt Clara!" Princess Sugar Plum exclaimed. Drosselmeyer looked at Egon.

Egon jerked his head sharply. Anyone else would have gotten whiplash. "He is not going to let me?" Egon bellowed. The rims of his pupils glowed as bright as a flame.

Princess Sugar Plum shuddered. She felt her shoulder blades against the wall. Sugar Plum didn't want Egon to sense the fear that was creeping up inside her. She said as boldly as she could, "You are no match for my brother. He beat you before!"

Drosselmeyer stepped back quickly, away from Egon.

The tips of Egon's fur turned burnt red as he pulled viciously at the handle on the chamber's door. Suffocating fumes of smoke thundered out of his nostrils. Egon yanked with fury at the door's handle. The door did not open.

Cursing and spitting, Egon pulled at the bars on the door's window. His tail slashed against the walls. Egon glared inside the chamber at Princess Sugar Plum. Sugar Plum was now shriveled up in a far corner on the floor. Egon pulled and pulled. The muscles in his arm bulged. The door still did not open.

Egon then kicked the door with his powerful legs. The vibration knocked the sconce next to the chamber off the wall. The sconce crashed on the floor. The door still did not open.

Drosselmeyer moved further back. Princess Sugar Plum half stood and looked around frantically for a way to escape.

Egon roared, "WHERE IS THE KEY?"

"I believe you took it upstairs after we locked her up," Drosselmeyer replied, rather calmly, not matching Egon's emotion.

Egon jerked ferociously at the bars of the window on the door, again. He looked like a wild boar that had been trapped by a hunter. The banging sound of the door being pulled from its hinges echoed in the small chamber.

Princess Sugar Plum cupped her ears and closed her eyes. *I will leap over them and fly out!*

Princess Sugar Plum's heart raced. Sweat dripped down her face. She stared at the door. She knew that she would have to move quickly to avoid being caught by Egon. *As soon as the door opens, I will—*

Egon held the bars of the window. His snout fit through the bars. His nostrils funneled smoke into the room, filling the chamber. Princess Sugar Plum coughed from the stench and held her nose. She looked at the door. *Please don't open.* She stayed ready. *I will leap right over them and fly out.*

Even with Egon's strength, the chamber's door would not open. The chamber was designed so that prisoners of Niedertrachtig Castle had no way to escape, nor could the doors be opened without a key. Egon continued to yank at the door's bars.

Drosselmeyer, holding his nose, eventually said, in a weasel-sounding voice,

"She is of no consequence to me, but getting rid of her now may hurt our bigger plans."

Princess Sugar Plum gasped, covering her mouth. She wondered, *What happened to Herr Drosselmeyer? Maybe he was always evil? Perhaps he was trying to fool us for his bigger plans.*

Egon finally backed away from the chamber door. Smoke was no longer coming out of his nostrils, and his eyes were no longer rimmed in red. He then adjusted the crown on his head and gazed once again into the chamber through the bars. "I don't quite like the taste of fairies, anyway. I prefer tough meat. Now, Clara—she's no fairy." Egon smacked his lips. His face was calm. The only expression displayed came from the grin of his piercing teeth.

"We must finish setting up," Drosselmeyer said.

Egon responded, "Yes, Dusty thinks that we are exchanging Clara for the little fairy princess."

Drosselmeyer nodded.

"Right into our trap," Egon snarled. "I should have just finished him at Konfetenburg."

Drosselmeyer looked at Egon. A hint of nervous tension could be heard in his voice, "B-but then we both would not have been able to get revenge." He added, "No, this plan is much better. We can both relish in sweet revenge, this way. I need—we need Clara to come here."

"Yes, she is the cause of the death of my brother." Egon paused. "And she will pay the price." Egon pulled his cape over his shoulder. He hissed as he and Drosselmeyer trudged down the corridor. Egon's tail lashed through the air. With every whip of his tail, the stench from his body traveled down the passage into the small chamber.

Princess Sugar Plum could hear the whipping sound of Egon's tail. She gasped as she smelled the stench coming through the bars of the window. *I must warn Prince Dustin and Clara.* She stared around at the walls. *First, I must find a way out of this chamber.*

-14-

The Chase

"Clara, don't move," Prince Dustin said looking around. There was an eerie calmness in the forest.

Clara jumped. They were surrounded. Clara's face turned stark white. She nodded without uttering a word. Her eyes jetted from left to right. Hundreds of the greenish-brown creatures were all around them. The animals rattled their tails and snapped their claws. Their eyes glowed green as if their eyes were bloodshot with anger.

Prince Dustin yanked his sword out of its sheath. "That other creature must have signaled the pack," Prince Dustin said, angling his sword toward the animals.

The General grunted. "They have been following us. They stayed back, waiting for us to reach this clearing."

Prince Dustin cast a careful glance at the creature that was at the front of the pack. It was bigger than the others. It seemed to be in charge, signaling the pack of animals. "They are going to attack." Prince Dustin said, almost whispering. Bronson nodded.

Clara looked painfully at Prince Dustin. The leader of the animals stared at him with vicious eyes, apparently not frightened by the glint of Prince Dustin's sword. The leader looked as though he was going to maul Prince Dustin at any moment. Clara's heart pounded, and sweat poured down her face. She looked around for something to use as a weapon.

"We must split up." Prince Dustin grimaced. "General, take Clara."

The General replied, "Clara will be safe with me."

"C-l-a-r-a," Prince Dustin said slowly, looking back at Clara. "I want you to walk to the path on your right. The General will protect you." Clara nodded, looked over at the path and then glanced back at Prince Dustin.

"Bronson and I will steer them away. They won't be able to catch us," Prince Dustin added, looking at the dense trees on the opposite side of the clearing. Clara blinked. Sweat from her forehead got into her eyes. Her eyes stung.

"Clara, you must move now," Prince Dustin said without taking his eyes off the leader of the creatures. Clara turned and looked at the General.

The General said, "Follow me, Clara." The General then backed up, toward the path on the right. Clara backed up without taking her eyes off Prince Dustin and Bronson. Prince Dustin yelled, then charged toward the leader of the creatures. His sword glistened.

The leader of the pack stood still, then hissed with venom. All the animals then hissed. They snapped their claws and rattled their tails as they moved toward Prince Dustin and Bronson. Birds in the nearby trees took off in flight.

Clara looked behind her shoulder at Bronson and Prince Dustin with worried eyes. She and the General reached the path on the right. Clara took one last peek over her shoulder and saw Prince Dustin jump over the animals swinging his sword like a club. Bronson followed close behind, not running on his hind legs, but on all four. Bronson had his tail raised high.

"They will be able to outrun those creatures, right?" Clara asked. She hoped that the General would respond, yes.

"Prince Dustin is a fierce soldier," the General replied. "He will not go down without a fight."

Fight. Clara's eyes widened. She hoped that Prince Dustin and Bronson could outrun the creatures and not have to fight them. *There's too many of them.* Clara shook with worry then turned and entered the trail. The General followed closely behind. None of the creatures followed Clara or the General.

◆ ◆ ◆

Prince Dustin shouted as he ran toward the trees, trying to get the attention of the creatures. He hoped that all the greenish-brown creatures followed him and Bronson, and not Clara and the General. Prince Dustin charged into the dense trees with full force.

Bronson roared, "I'll lead us through the forest." Bronson looked like a savage grizzly bear—definitely not like a beaver. His nose quivered as he smelled the way forward.

The greenish-brown creatures were close behind. Prince Dustin could hear the rumble of their feet bristling through the fallen leaves. It sounded like a small army, he thought. The hissing noise echoed off the massive tree trunks, sounding like thousands of animals.

Prince Dustin gripped his sword. He was ready to sling it at the animals. Bronson remained paces ahead of Prince Dustin. Although Prince Dustin was sprinting, Bronson kept the lead, sniffing the trail. "This way should be safe." Bronson tilted his head, without looking back.

Bronson and Prince Dustin weaved between large tree trunks and around boulders and fallen branches. The terrain was level in this part of the Black Forest. Prince Dustin ran fast. Sweat flew off his face.

Prince Dustin and Bronson were able to keep a safe distance ahead of the creatures. The hissing seemed to get more and more distant as they ran. Prince Dustin reasoned that at this pace, the animals would eventually give up.

HISS   HISS   HISS

Prince Dustin heard a hissing sound behind him. He looked over his shoulder and saw that one of the creatures had caught up to them. Bronson must have heard the hissing sound too. He slowed his pace, looked back, and glared at the animal behind Prince Dustin.

"Move back," Bronson said. He then charged, raising his tail. The creature was too fast. It jumped onto a large boulder, avoiding Bronson.

"This one's very quick, not like the other one." Prince Dustin lunged toward the creature with his sword angled. The creature was smart and fast. It rattled its tail and jumped off the boulder at Prince Dustin.

Prince Dustin tripped trying to dodge the creature at the last minute. The creature snapped its claws at Prince Dustin's face. It wasted no time. It then leaped and grasped the bottom of Prince Dustin's jacket with its claws.

Prince Dustin tried to shake the little creature loose, but couldn't. The creature held on tight to Prince Dustin's jacket and rattled its tail. Its eyes glowed green. Prince Dustin kept trying to shake off the creature. With his free hand, he grabbed the animal and pulled. The creature hissed and released one of its claws. It snapped at Prince Dustin. His claws were quick. Prince Dustin did not appear to hear hissing coming from behind the trees. The army of animals caught up to them.

Bronson's ears perked. He must have heard the army of creatures. Bronson ran over to Prince Dustin. The creature was still holding on to Prince Dustin's jacket. "On the count of three." Prince Dustin nodded. Bronson then jumped as high as he could in the air. Prince Dustin moved his head back when he heard Bronson say, "three."

On the count of three, Bronson swung his tail at the creature, swiping it off of Prince Dustin. The creature flew up in the air. It landed on top of a boulder. The creature still did not relent. It jumped up at Prince Dustin. Prince Dustin slipped backward.

"We have to hurry," Bronson said, pointing at the creatures behind them.

Prince Dustin raised his sword and swung at the creature, smacking it hard against the boulder. The creature then fell to the ground. The creature whimpered a soft hiss before lying flat.

"Finally," Bronson said, looking at the dead creature.

Prince Dustin heard hissing and looked into the trees behind them. He now saw the army of creatures. They were close. Small branches and fallen leaves trailed behind them in a cloud of dust.

"Follow me!" Bronson said, bolting through the trees on all four legs. The creatures were right behind them. Prince Dustin and Bronson were unable to run fast. The trees were much denser in this part of the forest. The creatures were small and weaved in and out of the trees with ease.

Prince Dustin looked back and saw the glow of hundreds of green eyes. The creatures were only a few paces behind. The leader hissed and snapped its claws at Prince Dustin. "They are right behind us!"

Prince Dustin knew that they would not be able to fight off all the creatures. He hoped that he was strong enough to fly now. He raised his body and drew a breath. Prince Dustin smiled with relief as his body was lifted off the ground.

Prince Dustin used his energy to lift Bronson with him. Bronson was caught off-guard and flipped backward. "I guess you got your strength back," Bronson yelled as he somersaulted in the air.

Prince Dustin cocked his head. "Hopefully, we won't fall back to the ground."

"Fingers crossed," Bronson yelled.

"I am not sure that I have fully regained my strength." Prince Dustin was only able to lift them a few feet off the ground. However, it was enough to avoid the creatures that were still chasing after them.

Prince Dustin looked down at the creatures. "Let's go back to the path that Clara and the General went down. We should be able to catch up to them."

Bronson said, "That's fine by me."

Prince Dustin could hear the creatures hissing loudly from below. Prince Dustin panted, out of breath, as they flew away. He was still weak.

❖ ❖ ❖

Clara and the General slowed their pace. Clara didn't hear any more hissing but looked back anyway. She hoped that Prince Dustin and Bronson were able to outrun the creatures.

"I smell a lake up ahead Clara," the General said.

"Okay," Clara said, but she only saw trees.

"It is not too far. Once we reach the lake, I will signal Bronson, so they know to meet us there," the General added.

Clara wondered how the General would signal Bronson. *I guess they have all kinds of ways to communicate in the Black Forest*, she thought. Clara recalled the purple butterflies and smiled. She was glad that she was now able to speak to animals.

"General, why couldn't I speak with those, uhm, uh, sort-of-green, sort-of-brown creatures?" Clara asked. "Now that I can speak with animals, why couldn't I understand them?"

"Only certain animals, Clara," the General replied. "Some of the animals in the Black Forest are not social, but predatory, like the wolves. Nobody can understand them."

"Not even you?" Clara asked.

"Not even me."

Clara and the General continued down the trail. Clara listened to birds singing in the trees and smiled. She understood the words of the songs that the birds sang. Clara sang along with the birds as they walked down the path toward the lake.

❖ ❖ ❖

Prince Dustin and Bronson flew low above the path that the General and Clara went down. Prince Dustin's eyes looked sullen and his face distorted.

"They shouldn't be too far ahead," Prince Dustin said with a strained voice. He turned his head slightly toward Bronson.

"Maybe we should just walk the rest of the way," Bronson said, looking at the weary look on Prince Dustin's face.

Prince Dustin responded. "I think I'll be able to make it."

"Look ahead!" Bronson said with excitement. He pointed down the path at Clara and the General.

The General must have heard Bronson. He looked up.

Clara was excited to see Prince Dustin and Bronson flying toward them. "They made it!" She then doubled back down the path to greet them. The General followed, his ears were perked, and his eyes were moving from side-to-side.

Clara met Prince Dustin and Bronson on the path and gave them a big bear hug. "How did you ever get away from those creatures? I thought you were too weak to fly? What were they? It must have been hundreds of them."

Without waiting for a reply, Clara continued, "And why do they smell so horrible? What was that green stuff, anyway? It stunk." Clara spoke without catching her breath.

Clara hugged Prince Dustin and Bronson again, without waiting for them to respond to her questions. "I am glad you are safe."

"I am glad that they didn't follow you and the General," Prince Dustin said. "But if they had, I knew the General would not let any harm come to you."

Clara glanced at the General and nodded in appreciation.

"My body is weak. I will need to rest before I can fly again," Prince Dustin said. "It took all the strength I had to fly away from those creatures."

Bronson sighed. "There was no stopping those little critters."

They talked as they walked toward the lake. The General walked behind them. His ears stood straight up. Clara did most of the chatting.

After they had walked a short distance, they all slowed their pace and looked around. They heard rustling noises coming from behind the trees.

"We need to make it to the lake as quickly as possible," The General said sharply. Bronson nodded.

Clara turned and looked into the trees. Glowing green eyes stared back at her. The army of greenish-brown creatures had followed Prince Dustin and Bronson.

"Clara, jump on my back," Bronson said with urgency. Clara jumped on Bronson's back. She held onto the fur on the back of his neck. Bronson then took off toward the lake, with Clara riding on his back.

Prince Dustin and the General dashed behind them. The General howled.

"Hold on tight, Clara!"

"Okay," Clara said, gripping tighter.

Prince Dustin looked around. The creatures had already positioned themselves down the path and were right on their heels. Bronson was the first to make it to the lake. He jumped in with a loud splash.

Clara hung on to Bronson's back. Water splattered in her eyes. She wiped her eyes with one hand then turned and looked back. "Where's the General and Prince Dustin?" she screamed.

Bronson said, swimming away from the shore, "They should be right behind us."

The General tried to keep the creatures distracted so that Prince Dustin could make it to the lake. The General howled like a wolf. All the nearby animals scattered or flew away—all but the greenish-brown creatures. They kept charging forward.

"They are going to get the General!" Clara screamed.

All of a sudden, the General attacked the creatures. He grabbed one after another with his fangs and flung them into the air. All the creatures then rushed the General. Their eyes glowed like green fireballs.

Prince Dustin looked back. He saw the creatures attacking the General. Prince Dustin then ran back to the General. He ran so fast, a trail of dust formed behind him.

Clara saw Prince Dustin grab a tree limb off the ground. She couldn't see clearly, but next, she saw smoke and fire coming from the tip of the branch, like a torch. Prince Dustin waved the torch at the creatures.

The creatures seemed to be afraid of the fire. The General growled while Prince Dustin waved the torch, keeping the animals back. Clara saw Prince Dustin and the General walk backward toward the lake. The animals hissed as they followed Prince Dustin and the General toward the lake.

Prince Dustin and the General exchanged glances when they reached the water. They then dived into the lake. The fire from the torch extinguished. Clara held her breath. Hundreds of greenish - brown creatures hovered at the shore of the lake. However, the animals did not enter the water.

When Prince Dustin and the General surfaced, Prince Dustin was holding onto the collar around the General's neck. Clara smiled.

"Whew!"

-15-

Lovely Ladies - Part One

The blackness of the night was encroaching on the day, as if it were sucking all the life out of the sky. The stars tried to twinkle, but could not. It was as though their little lights were being extinguished by some mysterious power. It has always been this way, deeper in the Black Forest.

Clara dragged her hand in the water as she rode on Bronson's back across the lake. She liked the tickling sensation her hand felt against the ripples. With her other hand, she held on tight to the fur on the back of Bronson's neck. Prince Dustin held onto the

General's collar as they swam. Clara saw the tired look on Prince Dustin's face and was glad that the General was towing Prince Dustin through the water.

"Niedertrachtig Castle should be on the other side of the lake," the General said. "We should be able to see the tower of the castle once we get closer."

"Tomorrow will be Day Three," Bronson added. "We have until the end of tomorrow to save Princess Sugar Plum."

Clara looked ahead. All she saw was water. *That castle must be a long way away,* Clara thought. The lake looked like an endless pool.

"We will arrive at the castle, tomorrow," Prince Dustin said confidently. His eyes displayed otherwise. His eyes looked worried.

"We may need to rest before entering the castle," the General responded, hearing Prince Dustin's weak voice.

Prince Dustin nodded.

"I should not have brought you, Clara," Prince Dustin acknowledged glumly. "Maybe there was another way."

"There was not enough time. We only had three days—I will help protect Clara," the General reassured Prince Dustin.

"I will too," Bronson agreed with a strong voice.

Prince Dustin attempted a smile. After a pause, he shook his head. "I should have somehow suspected that Drosselmeyer was evil." After a moment of thought, Prince Dustin continued, sounding confused, "How did I miss it? There had to be signs."

"Uncle Drosselmeyer was always so kind to me and Fritz. I never thought he was wicked. I didn't know either," Clara said, with her face lowered. She felt sad that her Uncle Drosselmeyer played a part in kidnapping Princess Sugar Plum. She felt responsible.

"I am to be King of Konfetenburg," Prince Dustin said, his face still lowered. "Some King I'll make, I couldn't even protect Sugar Plum."

"We were all caught off guard, even Queen Nordika," the General responded.

"... and I don't even know if Sugar Plum is okay. Egon could have–" Prince Dustin did not complete his sentence.

"We will get her back," Bronson added.

"Without giving them Clara," the General said. Clara smiled.

"I'm glad you brought me," Clara said. "I want to help rescue Princess Sugar Plum." Prince Dustin glanced over at Clara and tried to smile.

"Why do you think my Uncle Drosselmeyer kidnapped Princess Sugar Plum?" Clara continued.

Prince Dustin shook his head. "I am not sure why he joined forces with Egon." Prince Dustin stopped peddling his legs. "It just doesn't make any sense."

"Queen Nordika thinks an evil power took over Drosselmeyer," the General added.

"That's good–" Clara thought about how that may have sounded and added, "I mean, I would hate to think that my Uncle was acting good, but was always evil. I would rather think that he was good and became evil."

"Like a spell, Clara?" Prince Dustin asked.

"Yes, like an evil spell," Clara replied.

"Hmm," Bronson grunted. "There is a lot of evil magic deeper in the Black Forest, Clara." Bronson continued softly, "I hope you are right."

Prince Dustin let loose of the General's collar and swam independently. "Evil spell or no evil spell," Prince Dustin looked directly up at Clara, "I am not going to let Egon or Drosselmeyer harm you or Sugar Plum."

Clara flushed.

Prince Dustin continued, "We will surprise them. They don't know that Bronson and the General are with us." Prince Dustin added, "The General and Bronson will hide inside the castle for a surprise attack."

Bronson and The General nodded. Clara listened attentively.

"Once they bring out Sugar Plum–" Prince Dustin paused.

"We will surprise them then," Bronson added.

"I will attack Egon, first." Prince Dustin spoke softly as if the fish in the water could hear and would report their plans back to Egon.

"We will catch Drosselmeyer off-guard," the General said. "I will lunge at him and retrieve his wand."

Bronson added, "Drosselmeyer may be a wizard, but he will not be ready. He will be too surprised."

"Clara," Prince Dustin said. "I will need you to go with Princess Sugar Plum. She will be able to fly you away."

"Fly away?" Clara said concerned. "And leave you all with Egon? I can fight too. Remember, you said I helped last time. Remember, I jumped on Egon's tail. I am brave."

"Not this time, Clara," Prince Dustin said sternly.

"But, I–"

Prince Dustin cut Clara off before she could finish her sentence, "I need you to protect Princess Sugar Plum." Prince Dustin winked at the General. "Sugar Plum will want to help. I will need you to convince her to fly away."

Clara did not look convinced.

Prince Dustin added in a pleading voice, "So Sugar Plum doesn't get hurt. She will probably be very weak from being in that castle all this time. We need you to protect Princess Sugar Plum."

"Okay," Clara said. "I will protect Princess Sugar Plum!"

"Thank you, Clara," Prince Dustin said, sounding relieved.

Clara had a determined look on her face as she held onto the back of Bronson's neck. Bronson slammed his rudder tail into the water. Water got all over Clara's face from the splash. This time, Clara did not bother to wipe her face. She shook her face swiftly, and the droplets of water flew off.

The color of the water matched the color of the sky—midnight black.

❖ ❖ ❖

The mellow sound of a harp blended with the whimsical tone of a flute. A mist of white now covered the lake like a bride's veil.

Clara heard Miss Patti say, "Clara, please do it again. Battement tendu, soutenu, soutenu, pique turn, pique turn."

"Yes, Miss Patti." Clara nodded.

Clara lifted her arm gracefully. *Something doesn't feel right.* Clara then stretched her leg and pointed her toe, trying to move her feet to first position. She could not. *What's wrong*, Clara wondered.

Clara thought, *perhaps if I lean over a little.* She leaned, however, she still could not move her foot into first position. *Maybe, if I turn my leg a little more.* Clara adjusted her leg and leaned to the right. Then—

SPLASH

Clara slid off Bronson's back into the lake. Water splashed everywhere. Prince Dustin caught Clara by the arm before she dipped under the water.

"Clara, are you okay?" Prince Dustin asked, lifting Clara out of the water. He then helped Clara climb back onto Bronson's back.

"Who's Miss Patti?" Bronson asked, shifting his body so that Clara could balance.

Clara wiped the water from her eyes. "I-I guess I fell asleep. I dreamt I was in my ballet class."

"You slept for about an hour," Prince Dustin said.

Clara waved her hand through the white mist. "What is this?"

"I am not sure," Prince Dustin said. "Everything just got misty all of a sudden."

If it were not for the mist, it would have been pitch black. "What is that? Music? Do you hear it? Or is that just my imagination?" Clara asked with a sigh.

"I hear it too, Clara," Bronson said. The General nodded.

"The music started about the same time the mist appeared," Prince Dustin said.

Clara looked at the sky and jumped. She thought she saw something in the white mist. Clara didn't say anything. She didn't want to embarrass herself again. *It's probably just my imagination,* she reasoned. Clara could still hear the music.

Clara kept her eyes wide open. She noticed that the hair on Bronson's neck stood straight and the General's ears perked. Prince Dustin was quiet and seemed to be staring at something in the mist. Clara looked in the direction that Prince Dustin was staring. *He sees something, too. I didn't imagine it,* Clara thought.

Just then, something shot up out of the water. "What was that?" Clara shrieked. Bronson bucked like a wild horse. Clara held tight to the fur on Bronson's neck to keep from falling off.

Prince Dustin let loose of the General's collar and tugged his sword out of its sheath. "I'm not sure, Clara. Let's swim the other way." Prince Dustin said, nodding in the other direction.

Before they moved, another one shot up. Clara twisted Bronson's fur around her slippery fingers as tight as she could. Then another one shot up, and another, and another. The sound of the harp and flute got louder.

"It's a flute … and a harp, I believe," Clara said. "It-it sounds like a waltz. Just like the music in my ballet class." Clara relaxed.

Clara squinted for a sharper look. "They look like ladies." She added with excitement, "lovely ladies."

Prince Dustin eased his sword back into its sheath. "Whatever they are. I don't think they are dangerous," Prince Dustin said. He looked at the General as if looking for confirmation.

The General did not respond. Prince Dustin, Clara, and Bronson all glared at the General. After a moment, the General looked over at Prince Dustin and said, "They may not be dangerous, but I will still stay alert." He then perked his ears.

Bronson pointed. "I think I see a small island behind them."

"Maybe that's where they live." Clara's eyes glimmered with excitement. Prince Dustin nodded slowly, as if he were still skeptical. The music got louder. Lovely ladies continued to pop out of the lake, one after another. They moved in rhythm to the music.

"They are dancing," Clara said, excited. Prince Dustin looked sharper at the ladies.

Bronson said, "I think you're right, Clara. They do look like they are dancing."

"I think they want us to come over," Clara said. The sound of the harp and flute got even louder yet, as if they heard Clara. The lovely ladies were ever so graceful as they danced in the white mist. Clara thought they looked like swans in the lake. "They are beautiful." Clara's face glowed.

Prince Dustin looked at Clara. "Well, we probably do need to take a break. We could rest on the island, and then continue our journey down the lake."

"Y-e-s!" Clara said, as if she had won a prize. Clara looked up. All was black in the heavens above. There was not a star shining in the galaxy.

-16-

Lovely Ladies
Part Two

PLOP   PLOP   PLOP   PLOP   PLOP
SPLASH   SPLASH   SPLASH

The lovely ladies leaped out of the water like dolphins. They wore sweet faces like cherubs. Some had long hair that was either crystal white or jet black, their hair draped down their backs, almost touching their ankles. Others had brown curly hair. Their hair framed their brown faces like baby's breath, touched by the warmth of the sun.

"They are performing a show for us!" Clara's eyes twinkled like stars.

The lovely ladies spun and twirled. They danced like ballerinas. Their elegant arms moved gracefully, like flowers bending from a gentle breeze.

Clara moved her arms like she was dancing, too. Clara was not the only one in awe of the spectacular water show. Even the General appeared to be smiling. "Can we stop and watch them?" Clara asked.

"Sure. Then we will rest on the island," Prince Dustin said.

"They probably have beautiful homes on the island," Clara said.

The lovely ladies leaped and twirled. They swirled and danced. All were precise and in rhythm, as though they had danced together—for thousands of years. They danced and danced and danced—*The Dance of the Lovely Ladies*. The ladies then back-flipped into the water.

Each splash created a ripple of waves. The water droplets hung in the air before descending back down into the lake. The white, cloud-like mist was a beautiful backdrop against the black water. Clara thought the mist looked like the curtain of a stage.

Prince Dustin looked at Clara, as if he were looking for a clue that the show was over. Clara's eyes had not moved from the white mist. She was mesmerized. Her mouth parted and her eyes glistened.

The music then started again. This time it did not sound like a waltz. The beat was much louder. Clara jumped and almost fell off of Bronson's back. The tempo and loudness of the music caught Clara off guard, especially compared to the melodic sound of the waltz.

"Whoa!" Clara screamed. Fear and excitement could be seen in her eyes. Prince Dustin smiled at Clara. "The music sounds like a march," Clara said. Prince Dustin nodded.

Moments later, two lovely ladies leaped out of the water. They jumped so high that Clara had to crane her neck to see them. The lovely ladies danced and did somersaults. They did backflips and splits in the air. They moved smoothly. Clara could barely keep track.

"They are amazing!" Clara exclaimed.

"Amazing, indeed," Prince Dustin said. Bronson and the General stared with glazed eyes at the performance.

The lovely ladies continued their acrobatics. Clara held onto the fur behind Bronson's neck so tight that Bronson grunted. "Sorry, Bronson," Clara said, loosening her grip.

"I'm fine, Clara," Bronson said, with a squeaky voice.

The lovely ladies continued to dance. After a short while, they took a bow and dived into the lake with a big splash. The lake took the form of a canyon. Clara felt droplets splash on her face. As soon as the lake was once again flat, the music stopped. Clara's eyes opened wide with an amazed look and her skin prickled with goosebumps. Everyone was quiet, as if still in awe of the performance.

The tootle-toot of a flute broke the silence. Clara clapped.

"Even if I took dance classes for the next hundred years, I don't think I could ever do that," Clara said, laughing with astonishment. Prince Dustin chuckled. Bronson grunted a laugh. The General said nothing. He just stared at the small island. His ears were perked.

The enchanting tootle-toot of the flute got louder and louder. Clara and Bronson listened. Prince Dustin rubbed his chin. The General did not take his eyes off the small island. After a few moments, one lovely lady after another, popped out of the lake. They swirled in a circle around the small island. They wore chandelier smiles and gracefully gestured for Clara, Prince Dustin, Bronson, and the General to join them at the island.

Clara reminded Prince Dustin that he had said that it would be good for them to rest on the island before continuing their journey.

Prince Dustin stroked his chin for a few moments before responding. Clara leaned forward with hopeful eyes.

"Yes, Clara." Prince Dustin said. "We do need to rest. We will all need our strength to rescue Sugar Plum from Egon and Drosselmeyer. I might even be able to fly if I get some rest."

Clara was so excited that she again almost fell off Bronson's back. "Be careful, Clara," Bronson said, shifting his body so Clara wouldn't fall.

"Thank you, Bronson," Clara said softly, lowering her eyes.

Tootle-Toot   Tootle-Toot   Tootle-Toot

The sound of the flute coming from the white mist made everything feel very dream-like to Clara. She wondered if the lovely ladies had special powers like the butterflies. *Maybe they can make me dance like them,* Clara thought.

As they swam closer and closer to the small island, Clara imagined herself dancing and doing acrobatics. *Miss Patti is going to be surprised next time I'm in dance class.* Clara smiled. *I will be able to dance just like the lovely ladies.*

Prince Dustin looked up. The sky was still pitch-black. Then he looked at the lovely ladies, whirling in the white mist, like angels in heaven—except the small island was not in the skies above.

Clara beamed with anticipation as they swam closer to the small island. The closer they got to the island, the faster the lovely ladies swirled and twirled.

The lovely ladies moved so fast that the mist took the form of a funnel, like a tornado. The tornado mist formed a circle around Clara and the others. The sound of the flute was even more powerful inside the tornado. The lovely ladies continued to dance.

Clara could no longer see behind the thick, cloudy mist. The mist created a barrier around the island. *The mist probably keeps all the evil in the Black Forest away from the island—away from the lovely ladies,* Clara thought.

Clara was surprised at how cold she felt in the white mist. Clara pulled out the crystal stone necklace that Prince Dustin gave her last winter. It had kept her warm, then. *That's odd,* Clara shivered from the cold mist. *Why isn't it keeping me warm?*

The color of the crystal stone had turned from amber gold—to black, Clara noticed. Without any further thought, she tucked the necklace back underneath the top of her dress.

The fur on Bronson's back spiked as they approached the small island. Clara loosened her grip. She glanced over at the General. She noticed that his ears were standing straight up and his eyes were moving rapidly, scanning the island.

Clara glanced at Prince Dustin. She flinched when she saw that Prince Dustin had removed his sword out of its sheath. Clara felt a queasy feeling in the pit of her stomach.

The lovely ladies danced over their heads. Their sweet faces made Clara smile. Clara waved at the lovely ladies. They waved back at Clara, in unison. Clara noticed that the lovely ladies exchanged glances and nodded at each other. Clara felt welcomed.

Prince Dustin angled his sword. The General exposed his teeth, and Bronson raised his tail. Clara didn't understand why the others looked alarmed. The flute sound was even louder. Clara didn't think her voice would be heard above the music, so she patted Bronson's shoulder to comfort him. The General communicated something to Prince Dustin. Clara couldn't hear a word he said. Bronson grunted.

Clara leaped off Bronson's back when they reached the island. Prince Dustin and the General were in the lead. Bronson positioned himself behind Clara. Clara could only see a few feet ahead, because of the thick white mist. It felt like she was walking through a cloud, like she was walking in a dream, Clara thought.

Clara glanced back at Bronson. She noticed that the lovely ladies were behind them now. Clara thought she heard them laugh. Bronson grunted.

I will be able to do hundreds of fouetté turns without stopping, Clara thought silently with glee. She smiled thinking about the special powers the lovely ladies might possess. *And maybe I'll be able to jump high like Rupert.* Clara was always amazed at how high Rupert jumped in dance class. Rupert was the only boy in her class.

Clara raised her right arm gracefully. She pretended that she was in ballet class. She gently lifted her wrist and strummed her fingers softly, as though her fingers were strumming through water.

She followed behind Prince Dustin and the General, alternating arms. Clara caught a glimpse of Bronson. He was scratching his head, looking at Clara. Clara felt embarrassed and dropped her arms to her side, and began walking normally.

Clara, Prince Dustin, Bronson, and the General continued walking. The flutes were still tootling, and the lovely ladies were still dancing behind them.

Tootle-Toot   Tootle-Toot   Tootle-Toot

Then—Prince Dustin and the General stopped.   Clara saw the General whisper something into Prince Dustin's ear.   Clara couldn't hear what the General said but noticed that the General's fangs were exposed as he spoke, and his tail was raised high like a saber sword.

Clara noticed that Prince Dustin looked alarmed. Clara gulped. Clara wanted to turn around to see what had alarmed

Prince Dustin. She wanted to see what he saw, but she was too afraid to turn around. Clara felt her stomach twist in knots.

Suddenly the music stopped—the flutes stopped tootling. Silence was all that was heard.

Clara's heart pounded as she stared at Prince Dustin. Clara then s-l-o-w-l-y turned her head around and looked behind at the lovely ladies.

"No! No! No!" Clara screamed.

Clara's pupils seemed to be swallowed up by the whites of her eyes as she looked at the lovely ladies. Clara's knees buckled underneath her body. Her face turned as white as the mist. Clara was barely able to stand.

"Clara!" Prince Dustin yelled. Clara did not hear Prince Dustin.

The mist engulfed them.

-17-

KNOCK-KNOCK

KNOCK-KNOCK   KNOCK-KNOCK

Princess Sugar Plum knocked against the chamber's walls. Bright-red blood dripped slowly down from her brown fingers. The skin on her knuckles was completely torn off from her knocking her fingers against the stone walls. The pink layer of skin underneath had turned purple. Her white dress was dotted with red spots of blood. Her face was smeared. She grimaced with pain each time she knocked her raw knuckles against the walls.

KNOCK-KNOCK   KNOCK-KNOCK

Princess Sugar Plum had already knocked against all the walls and the ceiling once. She was knocking again, hoping that she missed a weak spot. She had to fly up to the ceiling to reach it. *There has to be a way out,* she lamented as she continued to knock. *I cannot let Egon and Drosselmeyer get Clara! I have to warn Prince Dustin.*

❖ ❖ ❖

"I am kind of hoping that Dusty doesn't make it by tomorrow," Egon chortled.

"Tomorrow will be Day Three," Drosselmeyer said in a sinister whisper, like a man with secrets. He swung his cape backward and pulled his rumpled top hat lower on his head.

"It would give me such pleasure to take care of that little princess tonight ... and she thinks Dusty can beat me. I'm going to chew his bones and spit out the skin." Egon spat on the floor in front of Drosselmeyer.

Drosselmeyer held his nose. "Uh, yes, however, tomorrow we can take care of all of them."

Egon cackled, "That's if they make it through the forest."

"Yes, I suppose you are right. The forest may do *your* job for you." Drosselmeyer paused. "B-but, Dustin will do anything to protect Clara."

"I'm counting on it," Egon bellowed.

Egon's face turned dark, matching his eyes. His face seemed to lose its shape. Egon no longer looked like a mouse, not even a rat. With all his facial features the same color—he looked like he had a blob for a head, without a face.

Egon's crown slid and rested on the side of his head. One of the jewels on the crown fell off, as if the jewel was frightened by Egon. Egon centered the crown back on his head. With his left foot, he crushed the jewel that had fallen off.

"We can take our revenge tomorrow, Your Highness." Drosselmeyer narrowed his eyes.

"I suppose." Egon blinked once. "But, first, I'll get rid of that little fairy princess."

"Tomorrow, you mean?"

"Yes, tomorrow." Egon cocked his head, and his crown almost slid off, again. It looked as though the crown was trying very hard to stay on Egon's head, possibly wanting to avoid the same fate as the jewel that fell off.

Egon tapped the tip of his nail against the side of his face. "Should I get rid of Dusty, after the little fairy princess? Or Clara?" Egon pondered aloud.

Exposing his sharp teeth, Egon continued, "I'll save Clara for last." Egon's teeth sparkled like porcelain china. His fangs glistened from being gnawed continuously. His smile got wider and wider. Egon was obviously pleased with his plan.

"Good, then I can—" Drosselmeyer dropped his eyes, without completing his sentence.

After a short pause in thought, Egon said forcefully to Drosselmeyer, "Then you can do what?"

"Uhm, then, I can get my revenge." Drosselmeyer's eyes flashed a sinister gleam. At that moment he looked as wicked as Egon, a matching pair of evil.

"I will have a good dinner tomorrow, except for that little fairy princess." Egon's face cringed, as if he were disgusted by the thought of the taste of Princess Sugar Plum.

Egon and Drosselmeyer laughed raucously. The sound of their laughter echoed throughout Niedertrachtig castle.

❖ ❖ ❖

Princess Sugar Plum shuddered. She heard an echo of frightful laughter. "I have to find a way out." Sugar Plum continued knocking on the walls—her little brown knuckles were purple and numb.

-18-

Eerie Voices

Clara's fingers shook violently in the mist. *This is not real! This is not real! This is not real!* Clara wanted it all to be a dream. She covered her face with her hands. Her heart pounded, she could barely stand.

"Clara, run!"

Clara heard Prince Dustin speaking, he sounded muffled, as if he were far away, and not standing right behind her. Everything seemed to be moving slowly. Clara was in a trance. She stood still. She could not run, she could not walk, she could not move. All she could do was stand still, as if she were frozen in fright. *What's happening?*

The thick, white cloudy mist was all around them like they were inside a womb. They could not see anything, not trees, nor flowers, not even the ground.

"Clara, Clara," Bronson yelled. Clara was still unable to move. She stood still with a blank look on her face. She looked like she was in a coma.

Seeing that Clara could not move, Bronson picked her up and flung Clara over his shoulder. Clara's ponytails hung down Bronson's back like actual tails on a pony.

Prince Dustin said with alarm, "This was a trap. We have to get off this island."

"This way, Bronson!" Prince Dustin raised his sword over his head and pointed it in the opposite direction. Prince Dustin squinted his eyes, as if trying to see through the cloudy white mist.

"Follow me." The General howled. "Just follow my howls. I will get us back to the lake."

Bronson said without hesitation, "We will be right behind you."

The General's fangs were deadly. His nose vibrated like it was ticking in quarter-seconds. He was picking up a scent.

"Bronson, I will follow behind you, in case I need to fight them off," Prince Dustin yelled.

"Ahhhhhhh-uhhhhhhhhhhhhhh," The General howled as he charged through the white cloudy mist.

Clara was still in a trance. She felt her body being tossed around. Bronson held her tight so that she would not slide off his back.

"You cannot run away from us." The voices of the lovely ladies sounded like a frightening chorus of high-pitched whispers. It did not sound like the voices belonged to living people.

The General ran and howled. He did not stop or slow his pace. Bronson and Prince Dustin followed the General's howls like they were wolves in a pack.

"We just want the ballerina girl," the eerie voices continued. "She is ours now."

Clara kept her eyes closed.

"Ballerina girl, don't you want to dance with us?" Clara heard haunting laughter coming from all around. Clara closed her eyes tighter.

"We are surrounded," Prince Dustin shouted.

The eerie laughter continued, "Ha-Ha-Ha-Ha-Ha-Ha."

Bronson said with a raised voice, "Cover your ears, Clara."

The eerie voices continued. "We heard your thoughts, little girl. Who is Miss Patti?" The eerie voice screeched, "That sounds like a lovely name. We would love to teach you how to do fouetté turns without stopping, ha-ha-ha, one after another." The evil voices would not stop. They kept taunting Clara. "You can live on our island forever and ever, ballerina girl."

"Ha-Ha-Ha-Ha-Ha-Ha-Ha-Ha-Ha-Ha!" The eerie laughter echoed in the mist.

Bronson said, louder than before, "Don't listen to them, Clara!"

The evil laughter continued, "Ha-Ha-Ha-Ha-Ha-Ha-Ha-Ha-Ha-Ha-Ha!"

"AGHH!" Clara screamed. She thought she felt something tap her on the shoulder. She brushed her hand against her shoulder blade, but nothing was there.

"Ballerina girl, I don't think you want to dance with us," the eerie voices continued.

Clara twitched and almost fell off Bronson's back, again. This time, she thought she felt something tap her other shoulder. Clara shook her head. Her ponytails looked like they were wagging wildly like the tail of a bronco.

"Ahhhhhhhhh-uhhhhhhhhhhh," The General continued to howl without slowing down.

"Hold on, Clara!" Bronson yelled, running even faster.

Clara continued to hang upside down over Bronson's back. She raised her head slightly and saw a shadow in the white cloud.

"We have to make it back to the lake," Prince Dustin shouted, following behind Bronson.

Clara assumed that the shadow she saw was Prince Dustin. The General sniffed and howled. He ran at a fast, but slow-enough pace the others could match. Bronson continued closely behind the General. Clara's head bobbed up and down. She saw glints of silver from Prince Dustin's sword.

"Are we getting closer to the lake?" Prince Dustin yelled while looking into the white cloud all around them. The General howled without slowing his pace.

The eerie voices continued:

"Don't you want to dance?"
"We could dance high in the sky?"
"I think the ballerina girl is afraid."
"Afraid of us?"
"Why?"
"Are you afraid of us, ballerina girl?"
"Ha-Ha-Ha-Ha-Ha-Ha-Ha-Ha-Ha!"

"NO!" Clara thought she felt something pull one of her ponytails. "No, I do not want to dance with you!"

Suddenly—the mist stopped swirling. The eerie voices stopped laughing. All was gravely quiet and still.

A single high-pitched voice cackled, "If you don't want to dance with us, ballerina girl—then you all must stay! NONE OF YOU CAN LEAVE!"

The chorus of eerie voices chanted, "You all must stay! You all must stay! You all must stay!"

"STAY–STAY–STAY!"

The eerie voices continued. "YOU ALL MUST STAY!"

The General stretched his neck and raised his head to the sky. He howled so loud, it sounded like thunder. Clara was shaken to her core. It was unclear if it were the chants coming from the eerie voices or the shock of the General's howl that frightened Clara.

Clara fell off Bronson's back.

Prince Dustin raced to Clara. He stood above her with his sword raised. Prince Dustin lifted his heels as if he were trying to fly. Clara closed her eyes tight. *Please be able to fly,* she wished. Clara then opened her eyes. They were still on the ground.

Bronson vaulted to the other side of Clara. The General was swift. Nobody saw when he joined them. They formed a circle around Clara. The General growled, and Bronson grunted. Prince Dustin stood ready to attack. Clara huddled on the ground between them. She clenched her knees with her arms. Clara heard the eerie voices continue.

"We are the Ladies of Tanzer Lake Island. Once you are on our island–there is no escape."

The white mist began to fade. Clara looked up. Gradually, the lovely ladies came into full view–The Ladies of Tanzer Lake Island.

Clara screamed. "They are not ladies!" Sweat poured down her forehead. Clara shook like a leaf in a storm.

Prince Dustin charged toward the ladies. The ladies merely laughed. They were not frightened.

THEN, all at once, the ladies twisted their mouths, and their eyes turned crimson red. The lovely ladies glided toward Prince Dustin with force.

Clara's heart skipped beats. She dashed toward Prince Dustin. Prince Dustin pushed Clara back. The General and Bronson leaped to Prince Dustin's side. Bronson put his arms around Clara, as if trying to protect her from the lovely ladies.

The ladies flew at them. Their red eyes flamed like fire. Their hair was gray and tangled. White netting that looked like a spider's web draped their bodies. The ladies moved like ghastly ghosts. The ladies headed straight for Prince Dustin.

"No!" Clara screamed and broke loose from Bronson. Before Bronson could pull Clara back, Clara ran and was standing next to Prince Dustin. Prince Dustin tried to push Clara back. Clara's crystal stone necklace flipped out from underneath her dress. The crystal stone necklace started floating in the air, around Clara's throat. The stone had turned black. The stone was so dark, so black, it could have been called a different color.

Rays of black light streamed out from the crystal stone.

The ladies moved closer. One charged forward. Prince Dustin used his arm to shield Clara. He raised his sword with his other arm.

ZAP!

A black ray of light emanating from the crystal stone in Clara's necklace zapped the lovely lady like a bolt of lightning.

Another lady then charged forward.

ZAP!

The necklace zapped the lovely lady. One lady after another charged. Each was zapped by the black ray of light coming from the stone in Clara's necklace.

The Ladies of Tanzer Lake hissed. They all then charged toward Clara. Black rays struck the ladies like a game at a carnival.

Zap   Zap   Zap

After endless strikes by the crystal stone, the lovely ladies hissed at Clara and flew away. After all the ladies had departed, Clara took the crystal stone in her hand. It was cool to her touch and sparkled like a black sapphire. Everybody looked at Clara's necklace with astonishment. After a brief moment, Prince Dustin said, "We must go." Bronson and the General nodded.

Clara smiled as they walked. She did not tuck her necklace underneath the top of her dress, this time. Within moments, they were back at the lake. Clara climbed back on Bronson's back.

SPLASH

-19-

Darkness

Darkness was everywhere—the sky above, the lake below, the forest beyond. The Black Forest was B-L-A-C-K.

They were far away from Tanzer Lake Island, but the horror was still fresh in Clara's mind. The General had said that he had heard about specters that hid their real form and motives behind lovely faces, song, and dance. Once on the island, they would expose their true physical selves and torture their victims throughout eternity.

Bronson said, "The crystal stone in your necklace, Clara—it must have special powers."

Prince Dustin nodded. "The necklace belonged to my mother. She received it from her mother, and it has been passed down to women or girls in my family for generations. I do not know all the power and magic it possesses. It changes color whenever it uses its magic."

"The color had changed to black on the island," Clara said.

"Yes, Clara. It used its magical powers to protect us," Prince Dustin replied.

"I must give this back," Clara said, pulling the necklace from around her neck. "This belongs to your mother. It is too special."

"Please keep it, Clara," Prince Dustin said gently, waving Clara to stop. "It only gets passed down to women or girls because the power in the crystal does not work for me—or any man. The power of the stone only works for women or girls."

"What about Princess Sugar Plum?"

"My mother offered it to Sugar Plum, but she would not accept it. Sugar Plum explained to my mother that fairies already had special powers and she would not need the magic of the crystal stone. Sugar Plum said that fairies could fly away from danger."

"But this is for your family." Clara added, looking directly at Prince Dustin, "I cannot keep it."

"I understand, Clara," Prince Dustin said sadly. He then looked at Clara with eager eyes. "Do you think you could wear it until my mother returns. Keep it from getting lost?"

Clara saw Bronson and the General smile and exchange glances with Prince Dustin. "Wear the necklace? Yes, I can wear it. I'll return it when you find your mother and father." Clara added with enthusiasm, "I'll keep the necklace safe!" Clara tucked the crystal stone necklace safely back underneath her top. Clara beamed with pride.

"Look ahead!" Bronson pointed to a castle in the distance.

"That's Niedertrachtig Castle," the General said. Although the moon was bright in the sky, only a dim glint of light from the glow of the moon hit the castle. Clara thought the castle looked like a haunted house from one of her storybooks.

"That is where they have taken Princess Sugar Plum. Tomorrow is Day Three. After we rescue Sugar Plum, we can save all the Black Forest from Egon and Drosselmeyer," Prince Dustin said.

Bronson stared at the castle. "I am ready."

"Me too," Clara said, although the thought of Egon made her shiver. Clara wondered about her Uncle Drosselmeyer. *I don't understand. Why would Uncle Drosselmeyer kidnap Princess Sugar Plum?*

In a short time, they were back in the forest. Prince Dustin had calculated that it would take less than an hour to reach the castle from where they were.

"Let's get a couple of hours of sleep before we head to the castle. Hopefully, I will be able to regain my full strength by then," Prince Dustin lifted his heels, but was only able to rise slightly off the ground.

The General replied, looking at Prince Dustin, "Yes, let's get some rest." Niedertrachtig Castle loomed just beyond the trees, like a cliff.

Clara glared at the castle. She thought she saw shadows dancing around the tower. She looked again. The shadows were gone. *My imagination.* Clara shrugged.

"We can sleep over there," Prince Dustin said, pointing at a big spruce tree near the lake.

Clara looked up at the tall tree and caught a glimpse of the moon. She thought she saw a crack in the moon. It looked as though a sliver of the moon was cut out, like a slice cut out of a pie. The glow of the moon was black at the point where it should have fully illuminated the castle.

Even the moon does not want to be there, Clara thought, glancing at the moon. *We have to rescue Princess Sugar Plum. We have to get her out of there.*

They ate berries from a nearby shrub before they sat down underneath the tree to rest. Clara looked back at the castle then drifted off to sleep. Prince Dustin and Bronson also nodded off.

The General stayed awake. He listened to every leaf that rustled and sniffed every scent that lingered in the air. Darkness was all around.

Down, down deep in the dungeon of Niedertrachtig Castle
Princess Sugar Plum was being held captive in a small chamber
with a heavy wooden door.
"I have to come up with a plan ... We can't let Egon get Clara."

ACT 3

-20-

Day Three

Clara was the last to awaken. It could have been considered late night or early morning, but it was sometime after midnight on Day Three.

Clara stared ahead at Niedertrachtig Castle. Shadows from the nearby trees cast uncanny moving images on the castle's walls. It made the castle look alive. Clara noticed that some of the shadows moved where there were no nearby trees. Clara thought the shadows looked evil, like an evil spirit. *I am brave. I am brave,* Clara repeated to herself.

Bronson glared at the castle. His eyes looked focused, even though the fur on his back was slightly raised. Prince Dustin had a determined look on his face as he gazed at the castle, although he kept pulling at the hem of his jacket. Only The General stood without flinching.

"Bronson, stay close to Clara," Prince Dustin said in a concerned tone

"I will not leave her side," Bronson replied, half bowing. The General positioned himself behind Bronson and Clara as Prince Dustin led them through the forest toward the castle. They each walked through the forest as if they no longer saw the trees, as if they only saw the castle. It was as though the castle was calling them. In a short time, they were at the gate of the castle's courtyard.

Clara noticed that the name, Niedertrachtig, was etched in the stone at the top of the gate. When Clara crossed the gate's threshold, Clara thought she felt something blow air into her ear. Clara hesitated and gulped.

"Did you see something, Clara?" Bronson asked, seeing Clara flinch.

"Uhm, no, it was nothing." Clara shook her head, although she was afraid, she was more worried about Princess Sugar Plum. Clara took her magical crystal stone necklace out from underneath her dress. *Just in case.*

They walked across the castle's courtyard toward a huge stone staircase. Clara looked all around and stepped lightly as though she didn't want to disturb what might have been 'sleeping' beneath the ground.

Nobody seemed to notice a flicker of light from one of the windows on an upper floor of the castle.

❖ ❖ ❖

Egon looked squarely out of a window in one of the upper chambers of Niedertrachtig Castle. "My dinner has arrived." Egon gnawed his front teeth until they salivated with drool.

A glint of satisfaction shone on Drosselmeyer's face. "Then it is almost time ... and after all these years, I will finally get my revenge."

"After me," Egon bellowed, not turning around to look at Drosselmeyer.

Drosselmeyer joined Egon at the window.

"And they brought that backward beaver and Nordika's mangy mutt with them." Egon flicked his hand backward signaling no consequence. He was apparently not worried about Prince Dustin, Bronson, or even the General.

"He should arrive soon," Drosselmeyer said, under his breath.

Egon glanced at Drosselmeyer and snapped his fingers in front of Drosselmeyer's face. "Dross—can you not see? Prince Dustin is already here." Egon snorted with disgust.

"Of course. Inside the castle, I meant," Drosselmeyer tipped his rumpled top hat toward Egon and darted his eyes from left to right. "How about we have some fun?" Drosselmeyer sneered, raising his brows. He then pulled his wand from underneath his cape.

Egon chortled, "Well it's about time you lightened up Dross. Yes, let's have some fun." Egon gestured with his hand. "You can go first."

Drosselmeyer waved his wand toward the castle's courtyard.

❖ ❖ ❖

Prince Dustin and the General were mid-way across the courtyard. Clara and Bronson were right behind them. They approached the huge stone staircase that led to the front door like they were visiting neighbors.

THEN—they felt a violent wind blow past them. Everyone stopped.

"Bronson, you and Clara go inside the castle and find Sugar Plum!" Prince Dustin shouted as he pulled his sword out of its sheath. The General stood next to Prince Dustin exposing his fangs.

"We will find her," Clara said determined, running forward. Bronson ran alongside Clara.

Prince Dustin and The General scanned the courtyard. Not seeing any clear threat, Prince Dustin charged behind Clara and Bronson. The General followed.

Within moments, Prince Dustin and The General were right behind Clara and Bronson.

Clara glanced back at Prince Dustin and ran even faster.

They all started running faster and faster.

Clara looked around the courtyard. She noticed that everyone was looking around. "What's happening?" Clara shouted, shrugging her shoulders.

"I don't know, Clara," Prince Dustin said. "Something's wrong."

Clara was panting out of breath but kept running toward the stone staircase. Bronson was still running beside her. Prince Dustin jammed his sword back into its sheath so that he could run faster. The General's ears were perked, and his tail was extended as he ran. They all kept running toward the castle.

The General growled, "The courtyard is enchanted." Bronson grunted in agreement. Prince Dustin nodded but did not relent. He kept running, although he must have known it was useless.

Clara now understood what the General meant. No matter how fast they ran, they did not move forward. They were merely running in place.

"Maybe if we move toward the side of the castle," Prince Dustin said, probably hoping that only the center of the courtyard was enchanted.

They all turned and ran toward the right side of the castle. Clara breathed a sigh of relief. They were moving forward—for a short while, anyway. Then once again, they were running in place, not moving forward. Sweat poured down Clara's face, but she did not let that stop her. She kept trying to move forward, trying to run free of the enchantment.

Prince Dustin quickly ran to the left. He was able to run for a short distance, but again, he was unable to move outside of the enchanted area. He paused for a moment then resumed running, "We have to get to Sugar Plum."

They were now all running around trying to find a weak spot. No matter what direction they ran, they were trapped inside the courtyard. Clara feared that they would not be able to get inside the castle and rescue Princess Sugar Plum. She did not think about them not ever being able to leave the courtyard. They were all trapped: Princess Sugar Plum, inside the castle, while Prince Dustin, Clara, Bronson, and the General were trapped outside the castle.

Although it appeared hopeless, nobody gave up. Everyone kept running. They looked like chickens in a coop. From above, they must have looked quite amusing.

After some time, they felt a violent wind blow past them, again. Everyone stopped running.

Clara said, somewhat surprised, "Did you feel that?"

Prince Dustin nodded as he walked toward the stone staircase. He pulled his sword out of its sheath and checked the space ahead of him as he moved forward.

Everyone watched as Prince Dustin was able to move toward the stone staircase. He waved for everyone to follow. Clara followed quickly with Bronson by her side. The General scanned the courtyard, as he walked behind Clara and Bronson.

Again, nobody seemed to notice a flicker of light from one of the windows on an upper floor of the castle.

❖ ❖ ❖

Egon laughed raucously as he stepped away from the window. "Well, I hope they still have some meat on their bones."

Drosselmeyer blew at the end of his wand, apparently satisfied with his display of magic. He then took a quick look out the window, not at the courtyard below, but into the horizon beyond. "Hmm," he mumbled.

"I built up an appetite watching them. Let's eat," Egon said, before marching away.

Drosselmeyer followed.

❖ ❖ ❖

The front door of Niedertrachtig Castle was ornate. It appeared to be made of very strong wood, possibly the strongest wood in the Black Forest. Prince Dustin noticed the details carved in the design. It may have reminded him of the Log Cabin Castle in the Land of Sweets. Prince Dustin looked over his shoulder at Clara.

Clara blinked.

Prince Dustin slowly turned the lever on the door. *CLICK* The door was not locked—or had been unlocked. "I think the element of surprise has been lost, so we will have to find Sugar Plum quickly."

It was dark inside the castle. Dim light glowed from sconces on the walls. The floorboards crept as they walked across the foyer. Prince Dustin motioned the group to follow behind him.

Clara looked into the darkness for eyes but did not see anything. *Good, no creepy green eyes,* Clara thought, relieved. Clara recalled the plan that Prince Dustin had laid out, "We will need to locate the entrance to the cellar. Sugar Plum will most likely be locked in one of its chambers."

They continued down a long hallway. Clara saw glimpses of pictures on the walls. Her nerves rattled when they passed a hall mirror. She thought she saw a reflection in the mirror of something—or someone. Clara jerked. She looked around high and low but did not see anything.

They continued down the hall. They reached a long hallway with doors and entrances. The first door led to the kitchen. Clara saw pots hanging from hooks. A stone fireplace was in the corner of the room. Clara smelled smoke, as though the fireplace had been recently used. An image of Egon, with his big belly, shot through Clara's mind.

Prince Dustin stopped at the next door and angled his sword. He turned the doorknob and looked inside. He shook his head and then continued down the hall to the next door. The next door was cracked. Prince Dustin kicked the door fully open. The door creaked. Prince Dustin shook his head again and continued down the hall to the next door. Everyone followed in silence.

Prince Dustin turned the doorknob on the next door. The door must have been heavier than the other doors. Prince Dustin pushed the door with his shoulder. He peered over the threshold. The door led to a staircase. The staircase led down to a lower level, the cellar. Footsteps from above caught their immediate attention.

CLOP   CLOP   CLOP   CLOP   CLOP

Heavy footsteps were coming from the floor right above them. The steps moved slowly, deliberately. Clara gulped.

Egon." Prince Dustin's voice was slightly higher than a whisper. "We cannot let him find Clara." Prince Dustin continued in a calm but direct tone, "Bronson, you and Clara go down to the cellar. Princess Sugar Plum should be in one of the chambers. After you find her, wait down there. We will come back for you."

"We will find Princess Sugar Plum." Bronson nodded as if saluting. Prince Dustin returned his nod.

"The General and I will lead Egon and Drosselmeyer away." Prince Dustin looked down the corridor in a steady sweeping motion. The General nodded, exposing his fangs. Clara noticed that the General's ears were moving like antennas. His tail stood straight out behind him.

Prince Dustin turned toward Clara. "Clara, Princess Sugar Plum will recognize your voice."

"Yes," Clara responded.

"Call out for Sugar Plum," Prince Dustin said. "I will close the door behind you. Your voices should not be heard beyond the door."

Clara nodded.

"We will come back for you after we lead Egon and Drosselmeyer away," Prince Dustin repeated.

Clara looked at Prince Dustin. *He seems different now,* she thought. She thought he looked many years older than fifteen. Clara would turn thirteen later in the year, on her birthday. Although Prince Dustin was only two years older than Clara, she thought he looked *much* older than that. *Prince Dustin looks like a King,* Clara thought.

"I will not let you down, we will find Princess Sugar Plum," Clara said.

"I know you will, Clara," Prince Dustin said in a calm and confident tone.

Clara turned and went down the stairs. Bronson followed behind Clara. Prince Dustin closed the heavy door. The staircase went black.

Bronson stepped in front of Clara. "Hold onto my shoulder, Clara. I can see in the dark."

"I am glad I can understand you now, Bronson," Clara said, holding onto Bronson's shoulder. "When we were in that cave last winter, and I had held onto your shoulder, I did not know what you were telling me."

Bronson said, "I understood you back then, but you didn't understand me."

"You had friendly eyes. I figured you had to be nice," Clara said. Sconces on the walls lit the corridor with dim light. An artery of corridors criss-crossed the halls "Those must be the chambers," Clara said.

"Yes, those are chambers," Bronson replied.

"There must be a lot of chambers down here," Clara said with woe.

Bronson said grimly, looking around, "This is not a cellar, Clara. This is a dungeon for prisoners, many prisoners."

Clara yelled, "Princess Sugar Plum, are you down here?" Clara hoped that Princess Sugar Plum could hear her. Clara tilted her head and raised one of her eyebrows. Clara and Bronson listened for a response.

They only heard silence.

-21-

Princess Sugar Plum

Princess Sugar Plum sat on the dusty floor in the corner of the small chamber. Her tree fairy hair was now a puffball of frizzy reddish-brown curls on her head from sweat. The ribbon holding her hair together in a curly bun had long fallen off. Her knuckles were sore. Her dress was now polka dot red from the dried blood that dripped down from her slender fingers. She finally gave up on trying to find a weak spot in the walls or ceiling. I have to find another way out and warn Prince Dustin. Sugar Plum had no sense of time anymore. Little did she know that she was too late.

❖ ❖ ❖

Egon, although a mouse, looked like a fat cat that had cornered a rat. He licked his lips and rubbed his palms together. His grin was wide, baring his glistening sharp teeth. His tail danced gracefully behind him, like a ribbon blowing gently in the wind. He looked up at the ceiling and rubbed his chin. "Should I roast that little girl, Clara—or eat her raw?"

Drosselmeyer swung his cape behind him. He pulled at his rumpled top hat. Evil could be seen on his face. "It is time."

"One thing, Dross," Egon said. Drosselmeyer seemed not to hear Egon. As if Egon was not speaking to him.

"Drosselmeyer!" Egon roared, using Drosselmeyer's full name.

"Uhm, yes, Your Highness."

"What are you getting out of killing Clara and Dusty?"

Drosselmeyer's eyes gleamed, but there was no smile on his face. "I am settling a debt that has been long overdue."

"Is that so?" Egon tilted his head but did not pursue the matter any further. His mind was already focused on something else. "I decided on chops for dinner tonight. Dusty will be my appetizer. You can have the rest."

Drosselmeyer looked at Egon with a blank stare.

❖ ❖ ❖

"Princess Sugar Plum!" Clara shouted. Her voice echoed off the walls of the dungeon.

"That's better," Bronson said, "she might be able to hear you now."

"Princess Sugar Plum!" Clara listened for a response.

"Do you think she is down here?" Clara asked.

"I hope so, Clara."

❖ ❖ ❖

Princess Sugar Plum perked her ears. She thought she heard something coming from the corridors. She lifted herself off the floor of the chamber and flew to the door. She could fly faster than she could walk. She pressed her ear against the barred window on the door and listened. Sugar Plum did not hear anything. *I guess I'm just hearing things*, she reasoned.

The opening of the barred window was small, but Princess Sugar Plum was smaller. "If I could just get these bars off, I could squeeze through," she said aloud, pulling at the bars.

After a few moments, Sugar Plum eyed the bars closer. *HUMPH*, She took a deep breath then yanked at the bars ferociously with all her might. "Come on! Come on!" Egon had no luck doing the same. Sugar Plum continued to yank at the bars.

What was that? Sugar Plum stopped yanking at the bars and listened. Again, she thought she heard something coming from the corridor. She thought it sounded like a soft voice. She peered through the bars. She did not hear any voices. She then flew back to the corner of the chamber and started kicking up the dirt on the floor. *If I could find a sharp rock, then maybe I could saw the bars off the window. Then I could fly out of here and warn Prince Dustin.*

❖ ❖ ❖

"I am beginning to think she is not down here," Clara said softly, slumping her shoulders.

"There're still a few corridors we have not gone down, Clara," Bronson responded. "Let's go down there." Bronson pointed.

Clara nodded and followed Bronson down the corridor. "Princess Sugar Plum! Princess Sugar Plum!" Clara yelled even louder.

❖ ❖ ❖

Princess Sugar Plum stopped kicking up the dirt. She stood motionless and perked her fairy ears. *There it goes, again. Who is that?*

"Egon and Herr Drosselmeyer," Sugar Plum answered as if she were speaking to someone else in the room. *They're coming.*

Princess Sugar Plum flew to the ceiling of the chamber. *They won't see me up here. They'll think I've escaped,* she thought.

"Princess Sugar Plum! Princess Sugar Plum!" Clara shouted.

Sugar Plum perked her ears. She thought she heard that soft voice yet again, call out her name. She cocked her head but did not fly down from the ceiling.

"Princess Sugar Plum!"

Someone is calling me, Sugar Plum acknowledged. This time she did not speak aloud. *It doesn't sound like Egon or Herr Drosselmeyer.* Princess Sugar Plum flew down to the door from the ceiling. She pressed her right ear against the bars of the window and listened. Her eyes twinkled.

The voice was getting closer. "Princess Sugar Plum!"

"Clara?" Princess Sugar Plum said with doubt. She grabbed the bars on the window of the chamber's door and peered through them. *That sounds like Clara.* Sugar Plum looked down the passage of the corridor. Fairies could see in the dark.

"Princess Sugar Plum!" Clara exclaimed.

That is Clara! Princess Sugar Plum said aloud, with a wide smile.

Clara repeated, "Princess Sugar Plum! Princess Sugar Plum."

"Clara! Clara! I'm here, Clara!" Princess Sugar Plum's eyes sparkled like gems as she pulled at the bars.

Princess Sugar Plum then heard footsteps clip-clopping down the corridor.

"Clara! Prince Dustin! I'm down here!" Princess Sugar Plum shouted as she looked down the corridor.

"Princess Sugar Plum!" Clara's face beamed when she saw Princess Sugar Plum's face through the barred window of the door. Bronson bowed.

"Clara! Bronson!" Sugar Plum shouted with joy when she saw them in the corridor.

"Princess Sugar Plum, we finally found you!" Clara ran to the chamber and hugged Sugar Plum through the bars of the window.

"We checked all the corridors," Bronson said. "This dungeon must have held many prisoners at one time. I am so glad we found you, Princess Sugar Plum."

Princess Sugar Plum smiled. "Thank you."

"Oh, Clara," Princess Sugar Plum continued, "you are so brave to come here."

Clara smiled. "You are like a sister to me, Princess Sugar Plum. I never could have stayed home. I could not let Egon, or my Uncle Drosselmeyer, hurt you. When Prince

Dustin told me that you were kidnapped–" Clara's voice trailed off.

"You are like a sister to me too, Clara." Tears of joy filled Princess Sugar Plum's eyes as she reached through the bars to hug Clara.

"We have to get you out of there," Bronson said, rubbing the side of his head.

Princess Sugar Plum looked past Clara and behind Bronson. "Where's Prince Dustin?"

Clara told Princess Sugar Plum that Prince Dustin, along with the General, was upstairs in the castle, and leading Egon and her Uncle Drosselmeyer away from the cellar. "Prince Dustin told us to wait down here after we find you and they would come back for us."

"Oh, no!" Sugar Plum wiped the corners of her eyes. "I have to let him know that Egon has no intentions of setting me free. He never planned to exchange you for me."

Clara gasped with horror.

"I've never seen Herr Drosselmeyer act like this before," Princess Sugar Plum said. "I don't know what happened to him. He must be under an evil spell or something. In the Black Forest, there is good and evil, and sometimes you can't tell which is which."

Bronson nodded. "You are right, Princess Sugar Plum." Bronson pulled at the bars of the window. "Let's get you out of there."

"I tried everything, Bronson," Sugar Plum said. "If only we could take off these bars, then I could squeeze through the window."

"That's no problem."

Clara and Princess Sugar Plum exchanged glances and raised their brows at Bronson.

"The bars are made of wood," Bronson said. He then smiled widely. His front teeth gleamed. "Beavers are good at gnawing through wood. It's what we do." Clara and Princess Sugar Plum laughed.

After a short time, Bronson had chewed the bars off, and Princess Sugar Plum wriggled through the opening of the window.

"Thank you, Bronson! Thank you, Clara!" Sugar Plum squeezed Bronson and Clara in a big bear hug.

"It was nothing," Bronson said, looking slightly uncomfortable by the acknowledgment.

"We must find Prince Dustin and the General." Clara looked down the corridor. "They will need our help."

"Yes, let's hurry," Sugar Plum replied.

Clara and Princess Sugar Plum rushed down the dark corridor. Bronson followed. None seemed to be worried about the evil awaiting them.

-22-

Little Girl

"Dusty, you're just in time for dinner." Egon smacked his lips. "I see you brought a friend, Nordika's mangy mutt." Egon cracked his knuckles and cocked his head from side to side.

CRACK   CRACK

The loud sound of his collarbone popping made Egon sneer with obvious delight. Prince Dustin and the General turned around quickly. Surprise could be seen on their faces.

◆ ◆ ◆

Clara and Princess Sugar Plum held their noses as they stood at the bottom of the dungeon's staircase. Although the door at the top of the staircase was still closed, the foul odor seeped through. Bronson had a worried look on his face, but the scent did not seem to bother him.

Clara's eyes stung from the stench. The smell seemed to be coming from the main floor. Clara had smelled that horrid scent before. "E-Egon is close," Clara said with a shaky voice glancing down at the floor, "and probably my Uncle Drosselmeyer, too."

Princess Sugar Plum drew a short breath and nodded.

"We have to get to Prince—"

THUMP

A loud noise erupted from the main floor. The door to the dungeon shook as if a great force had knocked against the walls of the castle. Clara jumped. Princess Sugar Plum's eyes went wide. Bronson ran from behind them and darted up the stairs of the dungeon.

Clara and Princess Sugar Plum followed Bronson. "What was that noise? What's happening?" Clara said, her voice was louder than usual. Princess Sugar Plum glanced at Clara with wide eyes. She did not know what the noise was either.

Yanking at the doorknob, Bronson yelled, "It's locked!"

THUMP

Clara and Princess Sugar Plum jumped. The thump was even louder at the top of the staircase. They almost fell backward. Bronson caught them both before they fell down the stairs. After gaining their footing, Clara and Princess Sugar Plum pressed their ears against the door.

Clara said with alarm, "Egon. It sounds like he's in the Great Hall. He's speaking to somebody."

Princess Sugar Plum added, "Prince Dustin. He's talking to Prince Dustin."

"I have to get that door open," Bronson said with determination. Clara and Princess Sugar Plum backed away from the door. Clara stared at Bronson with desperate eyes.

Bronson grabbed the doorknob again. He strained. The knob still would not turn. "Drosselmeyer must have used magic on the door."

Suddenly, Bronson let go of the doorknob and jumped back. His paw was seared and his fur singed. The doorknob smoked with heat. The heat turned the doorknob orange-red.

"Bwa-ha-ha! Bwa-ha-ha!"

"DROSSELMEYER," Bronson bellowed, hearing the eerie laughter.

Clara and Princess Sugar Plum stepped back. They glanced over their shoulders and were careful not to fall backward.

Why does Uncle Drosselmeyer want to hurt them? Clara hung her head in thought. She felt that it was somehow her fault. *Why, Uncle Drosselmeyer? Why do you want to hurt my friends?* The sinister laughter continued. It was as though Herr Drosselmeyer had read Clara's mind.

Tears welled in Clara's eyes, but not a drop fell. Clara listened to footsteps walk away from the door and down the hall. *It is my fault. I have to save them.*

❖ ❖ ❖

Egon grabbed another chair. As though it were as light as a feather, he raised it over his head then hurled it against one of the walls of the Great Hall in Niedertrachtig Castle. The solid wood of the chair kept the chair from falling to pieces. Egon seemed amused by the loud thumping vibration the chair made as it slammed against the wall.

THUMP

Egon sneered, "Don't you want to play, *Toss the Chair*, Dusty?" Egon shuffled his feet with delight. Prince Dustin and the General kept their eyes squarely on Egon and backed away. "You don't look like you're having any fun, Dusty," Egon cackled, moving toward Prince Dustin.

Prince Dustin held his chin high and did not blink. He scanned the room, as though he was planning his next move. Egon looked at the entrance to the room. Something behind Prince Dustin and the General caught Egon's attention. "He's back." Egon snorted with a laugh.

Prince Dustin looked over his shoulder. He caught a glimpse of Drosselmeyer's rumpled top hat and swinging black cape. Prince Dustin surveyed the room in broad sweeps. The General nodded at Prince Dustin. Prince Dustin acknowledged with a return nod, as if he understood.

The General then spun around and leaped behind Prince Dustin. His muscular body flung him through the air. Prince Dustin charged toward Egon. The glint of silver from Prince Dustin's sword cut through the darkness of the room.

Egon jerked, as if he were surprised, but not frightened by the assault. He then raised his sword and lunged at Prince Dustin.

The General howled as he vaulted halfway across the room. The ceiling in the Great Hall was quite high. The General soared toward Herr Drosselmeyer. Herr Drosselmeyer yanked his cape back and pulled out his wand.

The General's fangs flashed. His body stretched across the room as he lunged through the air at Drosselmeyer. Drosselmeyer looked at the General with a menacing grin. He then waved his wand at the General and chanted some quick words.

Prince Dustin yelled, "General, look out!" However, it was too late. Prince Dustin watched as the General was paralyzed in mid-air. The General fell flat to the floor with a loud thud. Only the General's eyes were able to move.

"Good move, Dross," Egon cackled, nodding his head with approval.

Drosselmeyer flipped the corner of his cape. "I didn't want him to damage my cape. I do need to wear this for the next hundred years."

Egon roared so hard his crown fell off. Prince Dustin watched as the crown rolled underneath a table. Prince Dustin then charged toward Egon.

Egon grunted as if he were annoyed that Prince Dustin interrupted his fun. Egon tossed his sword in the air, and then caught it. His sword was shorter than Prince Dustin's, but the blade was much broader. Egon then charged toward Prince Dustin.

Prince Dustin lunged at Egon with determined eyes. His sword struck Egon's sword dead center. A high-pitched sound reverberated from the clashing of their swords.

Egon was swift. His face looked playful. It was apparent that he did not see Prince Dustin as a threat. "You seem to be a bit rusty, Dusty," Egon cackled with a raucous laugh. "The object of the game is to disable your opponent. All you did was sharpen my sword."

Prince Dustin lunged at Egon again. Egon dodged the hit. Prince Dustin's sword ended up striking only air.

Egon's eyes sparkled. "Hmm, I think I'll bake mincemeat pie out of you, Dusty." Egon did a quick turn then lunged toward Prince Dustin with two lashes of his sword. Prince Dustin staggered backward, just in time. Egon only managed to swipe a button loose off Prince Dustin's jacket. Prince Dustin raised his head. Although they were blue, his eyes gleamed jet-black.

"I would love to invite you for dinner, Dusty," Egon teased, counting his claws. "Should Dusty be my dinner—or my dinner guest? Dinner or dinner guest?" Raising his fifth claw, Egon said, "Dinner!" Egon gloated. "I guess that resolves that." Egon then rushed Prince Dustin with full force.

Prince Dustin and Egon exchanged blow for blow, strike for strike. They fought hard. Sparks flew from the metal of their blades. Egon was no longer smiling. Prince Dustin and Egon continued fighting.

Prince Dustin panted. Sweat splashed off his face. His hair was wringing wet. His eyes were intense—he was not going to relent. They were fighting until the end. Red rings rimmed Egon's black charcoal eyes, as if he was under a spell. Grayish black smoke thundered from his nostrils. The smell in the room immediately changed. The room smelled even worse than before. It smelled like a den of a thousand dead rats.

Herr Drosselmeyer used the tail of his cape to cover his nose. Prince Dustin and Egon continued fighting in the darkness. Coughing, Drosselmeyer said, "I have had enough." Drosselmeyer moved toward Prince Dustin. He pointed his head at the floor behind Prince Dustin, as if he were sending a message to Egon. Egon nodded at Drosselmeyer, as if he understood.

Egon then lunged at Prince Dustin. Prince Dustin moved back. He missed being struck by Egon's sword, and almost tripped on a small rug that was behind him. Prince Dustin regained his footing and was standing on the small rug.

Egon then shot a quick glance down at the rug underneath Prince Dustin. Drosselmeyer pulled the rug from underneath Prince Dustin while Egon used his body to knock Prince Dustin on the floor. Prince Dustin fell right next to the General. Egon clamped his foot down across Prince Dustin's back. Prince Dustin could not move.

The General, still unable to move, looked at Prince Dustin. Prince Dustin looked back at the General. Prince Dustin's eyes showed that he still had not given up.

❖ ❖ ❖

"Hurry, Bronson!" Clara said, standing on the landing of the staircase. With eager eyes, she watched Bronson gnaw at the wood around the hinges of the dungeon's door.

"Just a little more, then we can push the door open, away from the hinges," Sugar Plum said, pushing at the door. Only a small section of the door was still being held by the top hinge. "It's almost loose."

Bronson continued gnawing at the wood. Within minutes, the right side of the door was completely free of the hinges. Bronson used the weight of his shoulder to hold the door open for Clara and Princess Sugar Plum.

Clara was closest to the door's opening. She bolted over the threshold and ran down the hallway. "They are in the Great Hall," Clara said without looking back. She waved for Princess Sugar Plum and Bronson to follow her down the hallway.

From the anxious, yet excited, look on Clara's face, one would have thought that she was running late for a party.

❖ ❖ ❖

Prince Dustin tried to grab his sword. It had landed beyond his immediate reach. Egon kicked the sword across the room. It clanked, as if it hit against something made of metal. Egon looked down at Prince Dustin and raised his foot. Egon then pounded his foot on Prince Dustin's back.

Prince Dustin moaned for a moment, flat on his back, he raised his head. His eyes scanned the room. Prince Dustin tried to swerve his body from underneath the weight of Egon. Egon adjusted and pounded his foot into Prince Dustin's back again, pummeling Prince Dustin.

Egon exhaled and thrust the tip of his sword at Prince Dustin's neck. Egon paused, savoring the moment. Prince Dustin did not move, from the side of his face, he looked up at Egon. Egon sneered down at Prince Dustin and then gripped his sword tighter.

"NOOOOOOOOOOOOOOOOOOOOOO!" Clara screamed and ran into the Great Hall flapping her arms.

Egon's eyes went wide with surprise. He jerked around and stumbled. Egon then charged toward Clara with his sword. "You little girl—"

Prince Dustin leaped off the floor, lifted his body into the air and flew across the room toward Egon. Prince Dustin flew so fast, Egon didn't seem to detect Prince Dustin.

Before Egon could finish his sentence, "You little girl—" Prince Dustin had used his body's energy to lift Egon off the floor. Prince Dustin and Egon were now flying, suspended in the air, above the furniture in the room.

Egon, surprised, hissed with anger. His sword fell to the floor. He thrashed his arms and legs in the air, trying to free himself from Prince Dustin's energy force. Egon cursed and spat, but could not break loose. He hung in the air lashing his arms and kicking his legs. Egon's tail seemed to give up hope. Egon's tail went limp and dangled down beneath Egon's body.

Prince Dustin looked down and winked at Clara. Clara laughed. Egon looked quite silly, Clara thought. Princess Sugar Plum and Bronson ran over to the General. The General's body was still flat on the floor. The General blinked several times as though he was laughing at Egon too.

Prince Dustin said, looking down, "Thank you, Clara. I am sincerely glad that you did not listen to me and wait in the cellar. You distracted Egon just in time." Prince Dustin also thanked Princess Sugar Plum and Bronson. Egon hissed. All seemed well for the moment.

Before anyone could respond, a powerful force entered the room, like a hurricane. Everyone turned with alarm. They had all forgotten about Drosselmeyer in the corner of the room. Even Egon looked perplexed.

Drosselmeyer swung his cape behind him and smiled. The force that entered the room was a man. The man was also dressed in all black with a rumpled top hat and swinging black cape.

"I knew you would come. This was all for you," Drosselmeyer exclaimed with delirium as he looked at the man that had just entered the room.

"That can't be," Clara said, stunned. She closed her eyes for a moment, then opened them. Nothing changed.

Clara jerked her head from one man to the other. "Uncle Drosselmeyer? Uncle Drosselmeyer?" It was as though Clara was seeing double. Both men looked exactly like her Uncle Drosselmeyer.

-23-

The Magic Spell

"DRACHENMEYER!"

Clara jumped. Everybody seemed confused, except the other man dressed in all-black that was watching from the corner of the room. From the darkness of the corner, his sinister smile looked frightening.

Both men were dressed in black with a swinging black cape and rumpled top hat. Clara looked closer, her jaw dropped. Both men were not only dressed alike, but they also looked identical, except for one thing.

Sitting next to the man that had just entered the room, Clara saw a dog that looked like Helmut, her Uncle Drosselmeyer's dog. Helmut barked softly at Clara.

"Helmut?" Clara said with a questioning tone, as if she was not sure if this was another Helmut, as well. Helmut barked again.

"It is you, Helmut," Clara smiled. She could understand Helmut. Clara looked at the man standing next to Helmut and rubbed her chin. Pointing at the dog, Clara said, "If that is Helmut," Clara paused, "then he is my Uncle Drosselmeyer," Clara said, pointing.

Clara then looked at the other man, the one that had been standing in the corner of the room all this time. Both men had gray hair, almost reaching their slumped shoulders and gaunt cheeks. Clara noticed that only one had a black patch covering his left eye.

"DRACHENMEYER!" the man with the black patch covering his left eye shouted. He glared at the other man dressed in black that was still standing in the corner of the room.

"Yes, I have been waiting for you," the man in the corner said. He then walked toward the center of the room. "Brother Drosselmeyer, I no longer need to pretend that I am you."

Egon cackled. He was still suspended in air, above the furniture, by Prince Dustin's energy field. Prince Dustin maintained distance between himself and Egon. Egon's eyes were now completely red, not just the rims.

"Drachenmeyer?" Egon went wild, thrashing and kicking his legs in the air. "I should have guessed that you were not Drosselmeyer." Egon looked at Prince Dustin and roared, "Let me at him!"

Drachenmeyer laughed at Egon. "You fool. I merely used you to get to my brother. I knew he would come here to save his precious, Clara." Drachenmeyer continued laughing.

"Enough!" Herr Drosselmeyer said, looking at his brother, Drachenmeyer. "It appears that you have deceived everyone, pretending to be me."

"And it took you all this time to figure that out." Drachenmeyer paused before continuing. "You were always, well, should I say, less cunning than me, the weaker brother, some would say," Drachenmeyer snarled.

"Weak? I am not weak, brother. I choose to do good," Herr Drosselmeyer said with his head held high.

"You are weak. People say that twins have a lot in common. However, dear brother, I never had anything in common with you," Drachenmeyer scowled.

Egon noticed that everyone was staring at the wizards. He then got Clara's attention and whispered, "Little girl, tell Dusty to let me down, and I will spare you, this time." Egon then flashed his sharp teeth at Clara.

Clara gulped.

Prince Dustin must have heard Egon because he shook his head and said, "I will not let you hurt, Clara!"

"Egon," Herr Drosselmeyer said with a commanding voice. "You will never be able to harm Clara." Drosselmeyer glared at Egon with his right eye, the one without the patch. "You have brought nothing but devastation to the people, animals, and creatures of the Black Forest."

Drosselmeyer continued, "You have ruled over your land with tyranny, malice, and evil. Egon, your rule is now coming to a quick end."

Herr Drosselmeyer then pulled back his cape. Everybody watched with wide eyes, following Drosselmeyer's every movement. Drosselmeyer pulled out his wand from an inside pocket.

Egon growled, and pointed at Drosselmeyer, "You don't scare me ... you sad excuse for a wizard."

Drosselmeyer raised his wand and chanted a few words. Everyone watched, nobody moved. Drosselmeyer then narrowed his eyes and waved his wand at Egon, casting a magic spell.

POOOOOF!

Everyone watched. Clara's eyes and mouth opened wide. Egon squealed as his body changed. His body started shrinking and changing colors. Egon kicked his legs and flailed his arms. His tail slashed across his back.

EGON'S BODY GOT WHITER AND WHITER, AND SMALLER AND SMALLER.

Everyone looked in amazement without uttering a word. Everyone, except Drachenmeyer, he laughed with amusement.

Prince Dustin flew back down to the floor of the room. His energy force brought Egon down with him. Egon was no longer King of Bosartig, Ruler of the Land of Mice. Egon was no longer big and threatening.

Everybody moved in for a closer look, surrounding Egon. Egon was now a little white mouse. Clara thought about Fritz's pet mouse.

Squeak   Squeak   Squeak

Egon skittered away.

❖ ❖ ❖

Now, for my plans. Drachenmeyer quietly stepped back to the corner in the Great Hall.

When Drachenmeyer was completely out of sight, he raised his cape over his body and disappeared. Nobody turned around.

❖ ❖ ❖

Clara said, slightly out of breath, "I have never seen anything like that before."

"I am sure you haven't, Clara," Princess Sugar Plum laughed. "I'm sure there are no wizards in your hometown."

Bronson added, "Egon won't be raging any more battles."

Prince Dustin shook his head. He glanced over at the General. The General was still lying flat on the floor. The General blinked with robust eyes. "Drachenmeyer paralyzed the General. He cannot move," Prince Dustin said to the real Drosselmeyer.

Everyone looked at the General. They all then turned their heads, probably looking around the room for Drachenmeyer.

"He's gone," Clara said aghast. She looked up at her Uncle Drosselmeyer with worried eyes.

"I am afraid he has not gone, Clara," Drosselmeyer said. "He has been planning this for a long time."

Clara sighed.

"Let me release the General from his spell. Then, I will explain" Herr Drosselmeyer then waved his wand and chanted.

Clara thought the rhyming words sounded like a poem, although she didn't know what any of the words meant.

The General started moving his body. He turned his head and stretched his legs. He then twisted his head and stood. The General bowed deeply to Herr Drosselmeyer. "Thank you, Herr Drosselmeyer. I am forever in your debt."

"Nonsense," Herr Drosselmeyer responded, shaking his head. "I am in your debt for joining Prince Dustin and protecting Clara."

The General bowed with his head.

Bronson joked, "I guess the General was a little useful." Everyone laughed, even the General.

After a few moments, Prince Dustin said, "Your brother, he looks just like you."

"Drachenmeyer is my twin brother. I am older by minutes. One can only tell us apart by my eye patch. I lost my left eye over a century ago."

Clara said, looking at the floor, "I am sorry that I thought he was you, Uncle Drosselmeyer. I should have known that you would not hurt my friends."

Princess Sugar Plum responded with sympathetic eyes, "He fooled us all, Clara."

"He is quite cunning, indeed. His powers are great. It appears that he has acquired more power since he was exiled."

Herr Drosselmeyer added. "I banished him from the Black Forest many, many years ago. Nobody was around back then, and those that were would rather forget."

Everyone leaned forward, listening.

"I blame myself," Drosselmeyer said. "His spells impacted the Black Forest for centuries. By the time I stopped him, it was almost too late. Evil forces had just about completely overtaken the entire Black Forest."

Prince Dustin said, "My parents told me about the Dark Forces that almost took over all the kingdoms. It happened so long ago that even they did not know the details or circumstances."

Drosselmeyer continued, "I did not want to believe it. I did not want to believe that Drachenmeyer was the cause of all the wickedness that occurred during that time. However, secretly, I knew. I could have stopped him before it got that far. I should have stopped him."

Herr Drosselmeyer shook his head. "I did not want to believe that my brother was evil."

Drosselmeyer drew a deep breath and continued. "I finally stopped him. I was able to undo most of the damage and banished Drachenmeyer. He was not to return."

Drosselmeyer hung his head. "I never let anyone know that I knew that he was the cause of the rising of the Dark Forces."

Drosselmeyer continued, "It became a secret. One of the many, *Secrets of the Black Forest.*"

-24-

Merlin's Magical Stones

Drachenmeyer placed the last of the three magical stones on the grounds of Niedertrachtig Castle. He was careful to place the Gefangnis Sapphires in a triangle around the perimeter of the grounds.

Gefangnis Sapphires had been hidden in the far corners of the world, centuries ago. Legend had it that Merlin, one of the most powerful wizards, hid the stones so that they could not be used against him.

The sapphires are said to possess powerful magic and can imprison even the most talented wizard, enchantress, or sorcerer.

"It is time, Big Brother. You will not be able to save the Black Forest, not this time." Drachenmeyer said to himself as he looked across the grounds into one of the windows of the Great Hall. The paleness of his eyes glowed under the moonlight. His face looked like it had no eyes at all. He looked as though he was not a part of the living as he moved across the grounds of Niedertrachtig Castle. Drachenmeyer waved his wand and chanted. Lightning struck across the night sky, and thunder roared!

❖ ❖ ❖

The light and noise coming from outside the castle caught everyone off guard. Clara said, "Something is outside." Prince Dustin withdrew his sword. Sugar Plum flew over to a window for a better look. Bronson grunted, and the General growled.

"Drachenmeyer!" Herr Drosselmeyer bellowed. He swung his cape behind him and pulled his rumpled hat further down on his head.

After a short pause, Herr Drosselmeyer continued. "Drachenmeyer is outside, on the castle grounds. I want everyone to stay away from the windows. This is between him and me." Drosselmeyer's face went stiff. He showed no expression.

Helmut pricked his ears and looked up at Herr Drosselmeyer as if he were waiting for a command. "Not this time, Helmut," Herr Drosselmeyer responded. "I need you to watch over everyone, especially, Clara. He may try to attack Clara." Prince Dustin raised his sword.

Clara ran over to her Uncle Drosselmeyer and looked at him with determined eyes. In her soft voice, Clara said, "I may only be twelve years old, Uncle Drosselmeyer, but I have learned a lot since being in the Black Forest. If you think he will come after me, then maybe I can lead him away from everyone else." Clara's eyes showed determination. "I don't want him to hurt anyone."

Princess Sugar Plum flew over to Clara and hugged her. "I'll go with Clara."

Prince Dustin said firmly, "Clara, you, Princess Sugar Plum and Bronson, stay here. The General and I will join Herr Drosselmeyer."

Herr Drosselmeyer bowed to Prince Dustin. "This is my battle to fight: brother against brother, wizard against wizard. I have to do this alone, Prince Dustin."

Drosselmeyer raised his cape over his body. In one swift movement, Herr Drosselmeyer disappeared from the Great Hall.

He VANISHED!

-25-

Wizardry

The castle grounds sounded like a mountain being moved. Trees on the grounds rumbled as the wind whipped through their branches. The windows of the castle rattled. One of the lanterns on one of the posts flew off and flung through the air like a cannonball.

❖ ❖ ❖

Herr Drosselmeyer raised the corners of his cape high and glared directly at his younger brother, "Drachenmeyer! Stop!"

Herr Drosselmeyer stood, suspended in air, above the castle's grounds.

Drachenmeyer stood opposite him, across the courtyard—brother against brother, wizard against wizard.

"Big Brother, I knew you would come to save your precious, Clara," Drachenmeyer said.

Herr Drosselmeyer responded, "It does not have to be like this, Drachenmeyer. Stop, I will give you one last chance."

"The power of the Dark Forces has been restrained long enough. I will restore their power!" Drachenmeyer cackled, and a gust of wind blew his cape high behind him.

"You know that my powers are far greater than yours. You cannot win in a battle against me," Herr Drosselmeyer said. The sound of his voice echoed through the grounds.

"Big Brother, do you really think that I would have gone through all of this if I did not think I would be able to overcome your magic," Drachenmeyer said, shaking his head. "Have you not learned anything in the past few centuries?"

"This is your last warning!" Herr Drosselmeyer raised his wand. "You and Egon will have fun together."

"You would turn me into a mouse, your own brother?" Drachenmeyer said playfully, as if not concerned. Drosselmeyer aimed his wand at his younger brother.

Drachenmeyer continued speaking before Drosselmeyer could wave his wand,

"You should not be so fast to use your magic on me. You may need it for yourself."

The lightning stopped flashing, and the thunder stopped roaring. Herr Drosselmeyer listened to his little brother but did not speak or wave his wand.

Drachenmeyer continued, "You must have figured it out by now." Again, Herr Drosselmeyer did not speak; he simply stood tall, staring at his younger brother.

"Yes, Big Brother, I have trapped you inside the power of the Gefangnis Sapphires. You cannot escape their magic!" Drachenmeyer said defiantly. His eyes sparkled like diamonds. Drachenmeyer added, "The Black Forest will be taken over by the Dark Forces of Evil!" Drachenmeyer shouted as if he were delirious.

Herr Drosselmeyer tilted his head and looked around the perimeter of the castle grounds. Again, he said nothing to his younger brother.

"And you will not be there to stop me this time!" Drachenmeyer appeared drunk with joy. "I have always been the stronger brother. You are weak and pitiful, Big Brother."

Herr Drosselmeyer lowered his wand. He looked at the tower and then looked directly at Drachenmeyer. Herr Drosselmeyer spoke slowly, "There is one thing that you did not account for Little Brother." Herr

Drosselmeyer paused and shook his wand at Drachenmeyer.

A grimace appeared across Drachenmeyer's face, as if he were wondering what he had forgotten. This time, Drachenmeyer remained silent. He wondered what he had missed.

"I too have learned a few things over the past few centuries." Herr Drosselmeyer flew toward Drachenmeyer.

Drachenmeyer looked around haphazardly. His wand trembled in his hand. Herr Drosselmeyer then aimed his wand at Drachenmeyer and chanted.

Drachenmeyer looked down. For the first time, fright could be seen on his face. He aimed his wand at Herr Drosselmeyer. Nothing happened. He could not stop Herr Drosselmeyer's power.

"NO! NO!" Drachenmeyer shouted.

Drachenmeyer watched as his hand opened without his control. Drachenmeyer's wand then flew out of his hand. Drachenmeyer tried to retrieve it, but the rod appeared to dance away in the air, toward Herr Drosselmeyer.

"Drachenmeyer, did you think that I did not know what you were planning. I saw a vision of Clara here, inside the castle. At first, I could not see the face of who held her captive. Then the vision got clearer. I saw my face—except, I did not have a patch over my eye. I saw you."

Herr Drosselmeyer flew closer and closer to Drachenmeyer. He stopped and hovered right in front of him. The wind blew his cape behind him. He then looked at his younger brother with sad eyes.

Drachenmeyer snarled, "It doesn't matter. You are trapped here, at this castle. You will never be able to escape the magic of the sapphires. Wizards more powerful than you have tried."

Herr Drosselmeyer stared at his younger brother and rubbed his chin. "Is that so?" Herr Drosselmeyer then paused before continuing, "There's just one small problem with your plan."

Drachenmeyer's eyes filled with hatred. "Even you cannot escape the Gefangnis Sapphires," he repeated, less convincingly this time.

"Ah, yes. Ordinarily, that would be the case," Herr Drosselmeyer said, pointing his index finger. "However, there is magic that can control the power of the Gefangnis Sapphires—a certain spell."

Drachenmeyer stood stunned.

"A certain spell. As long as it is cast before the stones are placed, then the stones will have no power over that person." Herr Drosselmeyer spoke with confidence. Drachenmeyer closed his eyes in disbelief, as if he knew what Drosselmeyer had done. "Yes, Little Brother, I cast the Spell of Stornierung immediately when I arrived," Drosselmeyer said. "It cancels out all magic that the stones would have had over me."

Drachenmeyer cursed and tried to raise his cape. Before Drachenmeyer could disappear, Herr Drosselmeyer chanted and aimed his wand at his younger brother. Drachenmeyer was magically lifted into the air. Drachenmeyer glided high above the castle grounds toward the castle's tower. Drachenmeyer cursed and cursed, but was powerless. He could not stop Herr Drosselmeyer's magical hold over him.

When Drachenmeyer was above the tower, Drosselmeyer tapped his wand, and Drachenmeyer dropped to the tower's floor.

Drosselmeyer then waved his wand and removed each of the Gefangnis Sapphires from where they had been placed. The stones glided through the air to the tower forming a triangle around the tower. Drachenmeyer was imprisoned in the Tower of Niedertrachtig Castle.

Shouts of joy came from the front steps as Clara bolted out the castle's door and ran down the stairs. Princess Sugar Plum was right behind Clara. The girls pointed toward the tower as they ran toward Herr Drosselmeyer. Helmut followed them. Clara hoped that her Uncle Drosselmeyer did not mind that they had watched everything from the windows of the Great Hall.

Prince Dustin, Bronson, and the General wore broad smiles as they descended the castle's staircase.

Prince Dustin looked up at the tower. He then rammed his sword back into its sheath. He walked tall, with his shoulders high, and his chin up, as he stepped firmly over to meet Herr Drosselmeyer. When he met Herr Drosselmeyer in the middle of the courtyard, he stood erect, without fidgeting. Prince Dustin no longer pulled at the hem of his jacket.

Looking directly into Herr Drosselmeyer's eye, of course, the one without the patch, Prince Dustin extended his hand. "On behalf of The Kingdom of Konfetenburg, and all the Kingdoms in the Black Forest, I would like to thank you."

With great flair, Herr Drosselmeyer grabbed the tail of his cape. With his other hand, he lifted his rumpled top hat and bowed. "Good day." Herr Drosselmeyer then disappeared. He vanished.

POOF!

-26-

Fireworks

It had been a day since they returned from parts *deeper* in the Black Forest. As Clara stared at the night sky above the Kingdom of Konfetenburg, she recalled her journey to the Black Forest last Christmas Eve.

She recalled being terrified of life deep in the Black Forest. Clara remembered jumping at every hoot, howl, and, cry coming from behind the trees. Places deep in the Black Forest no longer frightened Clara. *It doesn't feel that much different from my hometown. I don't know why it seemed so scary before,* Clara thought.

It did not cross Clara's mind that she was becoming more courageous.

Clara blinked, although parts deep in the Black Forest, felt like home to Clara now, she hoped she would never again have to venture any *deeper* into its woods, where few returned to tell their tale. Clara chuckled. *If I were to tell my tales to folks back in my hometown, nobody would believe me anyway.*

❖ ❖ ❖

Watching the show in the sky, Clara drew a deep breath. Her heart pounded, and blood raced through her veins. Shimmering shades of red, mixed with sparkling hues of blue, erupted across the horizon like a comet. Blinding light catapulted high into the night sky before bursting into sprays of glittering confetti. The dust floated in the air, before falling gracefully to the ground. Clara's big brown eyes twinkled with color as if someone were looking at them through the lens of a kaleidoscope.

An explosion of sound followed each stunning display. It was as though the sky was applauding the performance. Clara's skin prickled with excitement.

"That's beautiful!" Clara gleamed.

Prince Dustin, now King Dustin, was wearing his official, blue and red court attire with gold cords, bands, and buttons. A velvet crown of gold and ivory with blue jewels was firmly planted on his head.

King Dustin, Clara, and Princess Sugar Plum were sitting on red velvet high-back chairs, watching the fireworks. The show in the sky reflected off the stream of water flowing under the wooden bridges that connected the structures of the Kingdom of Konfetenburg, the Land of Sweets.

"I am glad–" King Dustin was interrupted before he could finish his sentence.

"Look at that one. It looks like a fireball!" Oohs and ahhs were heard from across the Land of Sweets.

"It sure does, Clara!" Princess Sugar Plum said. Both Clara and Princess Sugar Plum cupped their ears in anticipation. Their eyes blinked from the loud bang that followed.

King Dustin smiled looking at them.

Without any warning, the sky erupted into spectacular shades of color. Shimmering fireworks dazzled in the night: Stars and comets, weeping willows and waterfalls. Fireworks, in the shapes of flowers and horsetails, overlapped in layers–bursting without pause. Clara's eyes could not move fast enough.

BANG   BANG   BANG

The loud noise seemed to shake the ground below. Then there was silence. It was followed by a collective gasp.

"That was amazing!" Clara screamed.

Princess Sugar Plum nodded. "The best!"

"I am glad you enjoyed it, Clara," King Dustin said. He seemed pleased with the production.

"Yes, I did, Prince—I mean King Dustin," Clara said, correcting herself. "I have to get used to calling you, King."

"I have to get used to it, too." King Dustin smiled. Clara and Princess Sugar Plum chuckled.

"I wish my Uncle Drosselmeyer could have come to watch the fireworks," Clara said. "He would have enjoyed them. He takes us to see fireworks when we visit him around the holidays. They are not like this, however. This was amazing!"

Clara looked at Princess Sugar Plum. "I am glad that ... that was not my Uncle Drosselmeyer that had done all those bad things. I never knew he had a twin brother. Drachenmeyer is wicked."

Princess Sugar Plum responded, "We did not know he had a twin brother, either. Drachenmeyer is quite wicked indeed."

"He planned to restore the powers of the Dark Forces. It would have devastated all the Kingdoms, and evil would have prevailed," King Dustin said. "Clara, you were brave to venture deeper in the Black Forest to help rescue Princess Sugar Plum. And you distracted Egon, just in time. You saved me from Egon, Clara. I am alive because of your bravery. The Kingdom of Konfetenburg will always be in your debt."

Clara lowered her eyes. She didn't feel as though she did much at all.

"Queen Nordika has a surprise for you, Clara," King Dustin said. "She's waiting for us inside."

❖ ❖ ❖

Clara, King Dustin, and Princess Sugar Plum entered the Grand Hall of the Log Cabin Castle. King Dustin's coronation had ended hours earlier, but the smell of baked apples from the apfelkuchen apple cake still lingered. Covered plates of pastries and treats were all around, this was actually typical for any day, in the Land of Sweets.

Queen Nordika stood by a window in the Grand Hall. She held a small white wicker basket. Clara's knees almost buckled as she walked across the floor to greet the Snow Queen. Clara hoped that one day, she would grow up to be as brave as Queen Nordika.

"Clara," Queen Nordika said. "I have a gift for you." Queen Nordika lifted the small white wicker basket. Something in the basket moved. It seemed to be tossing and turning, shaking the basket.

Clara's eyes sparkled with wonder.

"It is a special gift, Clara," Queen Nordika added. "You have, once again, displayed great bravery."

Clara lowered her eyes and swallowed.

Queen Nordika smiled and lifted Clara's chin. She then handed the wicker basket to Clara. "This is for you, Clara ... for being brave."

"Thank you, Queen Nordika." Clara curtsied. She smiled with the widest of grins as she peered into the small wicker basket with wide eyes. Gold satin cloth covered its content. "It's moving!" Clara said with excitement. *What could it be?* Clara thought, anxious.

Clara gently lifted the gold satin cloth. Her eyes widened. Princess Sugar Plum smiled at King Dustin as though she already knew what was inside the basket. Clara raised the last piece of satin. Her face flushed.

"A little General puppy!" Clara exclaimed. A fluffy white puppy with small black pebble eyes and a little pink tongue popped its head out from underneath the gold satin cloth.

"—just like the ones at the Ice Palace," Clara said as she gently lifted the puppy out of the wicker basket and hugged it. The white shepherd puppy licked Clara's nose.

"He's adorable, Clara," Princess Sugar Plum said, rubbing the puppy behind its ears.

"I love him, Queen Nordika. Thank you so much!" Clara continued to hug the puppy and didn't seem to mind being licked all over her face.

Princess Sugar Plum said, "You have to give the puppy a name, Clara."

"Yes ... I have to name him—or is it a her?" Clara said, sounding confused.

Queen Nordika said, "You're correct, Clara. It is a he."

Clara lifted the puppy to her face and looked into its eyes. "What should I name you?"

A big smile spread across Clara's face. "I am going to name you, Mozart. His music is my favorite!"

❖ ❖ ❖

The next morning, Clara, King Dustin, and Princess Sugar sailed across the sky back to Clara's hometown. Clara held the white wicker basket close to her chest. The rocking from their flight must have made the little puppy drift off to sleep inside the basket. The basket did not rock or move.

Clara noticed that Princess Sugar Plum flew much faster across the sky than King Dustin. Princess Sugar Plum had told Clara that since she was an actual tree fairy, she could fly at top speeds. Sugar Plum had explained that since King Dustin was granted the ability to fly, and was not a tree fairy, he could not fly nearly as fast as fairies. With

Sugar Plum's energy force, they whipped through the skies like a shooting star.

In less than an hour, Clara was back home. It was still early in the morning.

Clara, King Dustin, and Princess Sugar Plum whispered and laughed softly in Clara's bedroom. Hearing someone approach, King Dustin and Princess Sugar Plum hugged Clara and patted Mozart on the top of his head.

"We look forward to seeing you again, Clara," King Dustin said. He and Princess Sugar Plum then flew out of Clara's bedroom window.

Clara smiled. She wondered if she would see them again, soon—or sometime in the far future.

Knock-Knock

"Clara?" Fritz said, knocking on Clara's bedroom door.

"One moment, Fritz," Clara responded quickly. Clara placed Mozart inside the wicker basket and covered him with the gold satin cloth. Clara then walked across the room and opened the door. Fritz bolted in the room, excited to see Clara.

"When did you get back?"

Clara gulped. "I, uhm—"

Fritz continued, "I thought you weren't coming back from Marie's house until tomorrow."

"Uhm ... oh, yes," Clara rubbed her eyelid. "I missed you Fritz, so I decided to come back a day early."

Fritz pulled his mouth to one side and looked at Clara with doubtful eyes.

"Did you and Bruno have a good time? You stayed out of trouble, didn't you?" Clara asked, changing the subject.

"Of course, Clara. We stayed out of trouble," Fritz said.

This time Clara pulled her mouth to one side and looked at Fritz with doubtful eyes.

"Well, mostly," Fritz said laughing.

Clara smiled. She noticed the tail of Fritz's pet mouse dangling back and forth from the pocket of his shirt.

Just then—the wicker basket moved. It shook from side to side. It almost toppled over on Clara's bed.

"What's that?" Fritz said in a curious tone, pointing at the wicker basket.

"Oh, it's nothing," Clara said. Clara stood and motioned Fritz toward the door. "It's probably time for breakf—"

Before Clara could finish her sentence, Mozart jumped out of the wicker basket onto Clara's bed.

"Clara! You have a dog!" Fritz screamed. "Come here, boy." Fritz whistled.

"It's a puppy," Clara responded.

"Can I play with him, Clara?" Fritz said with pleading eyes.

Clara looked at Mozart, then back at Fritz. "I will let you play with him, later, maybe."

"Oh, Clara, please!" Fritz looked at Clara with that innocent look.

"Okay, after breakfast," Clara said. "Now go."

Clara closed her bedroom door behind Fritz. She then sat down on her bed and lifted the puppy to her face. Clara looked into the puppy's black pebble eyes and said, "I will make sure that Fritz doesn't hurt you, Mozart."

Mozart barked, "He seems like fun, Clara."

Clara's jaw dropped. She forgot that she could now speak with animals.

The End

Resources & Notes

Daniel Lee Nicholson selected the Black Forest, Germany, as the setting for the book series, **Prince Dustin and Clara**, because of its proximity to the original setting of the ballet, **The Nutcracker**. The original ballet was based on Alexandre Dumas' retelling of ETA Hoffman's classic tale, *The Nutcracker and the Mouse King*.

In addition to history and culture, the Black Forest is rich in legends and folklore, making it an alluring place for enchantment, or a magical setting for a fairy tale. The first installment in the series, **Deep in the Black Forest**, retells the story of The Nutcracker ballet with a re-imagining of the Snow Scene. Unlike the ballet, where the snow scene is about 18 minutes, in Book One of the series, the snow scene comprises most of the book, 13 adventurous chapters.

Our stories are divided into acts, just like a ballet. In addition to the performing arts: dance and music, Fossil Mountain Publishing strives to include the fine arts in its books. Our books include cover illustrations that can be appreciated for their aesthetic appeal, in addition to providing a visual of the artist's interpretation of a scene from the book. Interior artwork includes detailed sketches, with captions, and are framed in elaborate borders, as if the sketches were hanging on the walls in an art gallery.

Nicholson chose the characters' names and many of the names of the animals and places based on their general meaning and definition. Many words are from the German language or have a German association. One exception is the name of Clara's dance teacher in the book, *Miss Patti*. That name was chosen in homage to Daniel Lee Nicholson's first ballet instructor in Chicago.

We hope you have enjoyed Book Two, ***Prince Dustin and Clara: Secrets of the Black Forest***, and will tell your family and friends about the series. Book Three in the series, ***Prince Dustin and Clara: Escape from the Black Forest***, promises even more magic, fantasy, and thrills—*and maybe a few surprises!*

❖ ❖ ❖

As beneficiaries of *The Arts*, we at Fossil Mountain Publishing know the difference an education including *The Arts* can have on a person's life. Therefore, we would like to say thank you for your continued support of *The Arts*!

*"**There is no limit to what a person can do that has been inspired by The Arts!**"*
—Fossil Mountain Publishing, LLC

About Us

Author
Daniel Lee Nicholson was born and raised in the Midwest. He has been a performer and ambassador of the performing and fine arts ever since his first performance as a soldier in *The Nutcracker* in Chicago. Nicholson performed in various productions of *The Nutcracker* ballet spanning 10 years. He currently resides with his wife in the Los Angeles area and works in the Media and Entertainment industry.

Publisher
The mission of Fossil Mountain Publishing LLC is to captivate and entertain; engage and inspire young readers and readers of all ages by publishing family-oriented books that promote reading and literature; technology and *The Arts*. We strive to develop applications and to incorporate technology into our platforms so that our readers can fully immerse themselves in great stories.
– Visit us at
www.FossilMountainPublishing.com

❖ ❖ ❖

ARTISTS
Cover Illustrator:
  Nele Diel, www.nelediel.com (Germany)
Cover Designer, Interior Artwork:
  Luke Ahearn, www.reedsy.com/luke-ahearn

CPSIA information can be obtained
at www.ICGtesting.com
Printed in the USA
FSHW010148020919
61655FS